Walking for a Kiss

Thank you for reading my story.

Jared J. Reed

Walking for a Kiss

by Harold J Reed

PALMETTO

P U B L I S H I N G

Charleston, SC

www.PalmettoPublishing.com

Copyright © 2023 by Harold J Reed

Paperback ISBN: 979-8-8229-2667-7

Chapter 1

As seventeen-year-old Trevor Tremaine looked into the mirror, he did not like the person looking back at him. Ever since he could remember, he had been schooled in playing the piano, dancing, martial arts, and study. He had an exceptionally high IQ and his parents had taken every opportunity to assure he received the best education possible. His parents were quite wealthy and traveled the world, leaving his care to an aunt living in Cambridge, Massachusetts. As a master pianist traveling the world at age fifteen, Trevor had seen most of the major cities in North America and many of the capitals of Europe. It had been a rewarding experience, but it was losing its excitement— playing the same program every night over and over had become boring.

Trevor was also an MIT graduate at the age of sixteen, with degrees in electronics and mathematics. He had managed to obtain patents on several components associated with solar panels and other electronic devices, which assured him that he would have enough revenue to last a lifetime.

However, the face looking back at him was that of a nerd, with neither social skills nor the ability to communicate with others outside his extremely small circle of nerdy friends. Girls were especially confusing to him. If a girl even looked at him, he turned to jelly and became a super nerd. He realized that he had to change his life if he did not want to be a social outcast, having nothing in common with ordinary folks and the everyday lives they led.

Trevor spent the next two weeks thinking about what he wanted to do and how to go about accomplishing his objective. He had been reading a western magazine about ranch life and it seemed to offer what he was looking for. Yes—he decided he was going to look for work on a cattle ranch to learn what hard work was all about and to determine if he could feel rewarded by simple, hard work.

He also wanted to be outside more. He wanted to learn how ordinary people lived, as he had been pampered all his life. He wanted to learn more about horses, cattle, and being a rancher.

The most important points would be to learn to talk comfortably with people, especially girls, as they scared him to death. Trevor had never gone to a social dance with actual people participating. He also wanted to learn to ride a horse and to dance comfortably with girls. He had been trained in all types of dances all of his life, specializing in the waltz, but that was always with teachers. He would also like to take care of himself, as he had always been pampered and looked after by adults. At the young age of seventeen, he knew it might be difficult to obtain work, but he was going to try.

Reviewing the *World Express Newspaper* revealed that the Skyline Ranch, (a dude ranch, just outside of Casper, Wyoming) was looking for help with cleaning out barns and brushing down horses. It did not pay much, but it did offer room and board.

Trevor thought he would give it a try, as he figured out that it would probably be difficult for the ranch to find someone willing to work under those conditions. It would give him a chance to socialize with a variety of people and to be outdoors. It sounded perfect. Trevor bought an airline ticket to Casper and planed on hitchhiking the twenty miles necessary to get to the turnoff to the ranch. He felt this experience would be the beginning of his new life adventure. Luckily, he got picked up relatively soon by John Fargo, who owned the ranch adjacent to the Skyline Ranch property. John's seventeen-year-old daughter, Susan, was also in the cab with John, so they had to scrunch together for the ride—this definitely made Trevor uncomfortable and probably made Susan feel the same way, as they were the same age. Introductions were made as soon as Trevor was in the cab of the pickup, and they proceeded down the road.

Trevor told John Fargo what he was hoping to accomplish by his visit to the dude ranch, and other small talk was exchanged until they reached the turn off to Skyline Ranch.

John said, "Now you're going to have to walk from here as we are heading straight on down the road to our place, the Running Water Ranch. It's about a two-mile walk. If you cannot find work at the dude ranch, you might come over to my ranch—I might be able to find some part time work for you." Trevor said, "Thank you," and got out of the pickup.

Susan had not spoken a word during the whole trip. Susan asked her dad why he would offer Trevor a job at their ranch, as they did not know anything about him. Her dad replied, "If that young man is willing to hitch a ride out in this country and then walk a couple of miles to see if he can get a job that pays almost nothing, he seems like the kind of fella that deserves a break. We will see what happens." Susan was not happy with her dad's explanation but had no more to say on the subject.

Things did not go well at the Skyline Ranch. The owner, Jack Barnes, felt Trevor was too young and inexperienced to be around the guests that came to the ranch. Trevor thanked him for the opportunity to talk with him, intending to start walking back down the road after getting directions to the Running Water Ranch. He was going to talk with John Fargo about the part time work he had mentioned in the pickup.

The owner of the Skyline Ranch said to hold up, as he wanted to call Mr. Fargo before Trevor decided to leave the Skyline Ranch. Jack Barnes, after talking with John Fargo, decided to give Trevor a ride to the Running Water Ranch—it was getting too late in the evening for Trevor to walk that far before dark. Trevor took this as a good sign that he might get the part-time job; otherwise, why would he be getting the ride if he was just going to be told there was no work available?

As they were approaching the Running Water Ranch, Trevor could see a rather large ranch house with a large barn and several corrals containing both cattle and horses. Trevor noticed there were several heads of cattle in the surrounding fields as they traveled down the dusty road toward the ranch house.

Trevor thanked Jack Barnes for the ride before getting out of the pickup. As he drove off, John Fargo came out of the screen door onto the front of the wraparound porch. Susan was sitting on the far end of the porch with a blanket hanging loosely over her lap. Trevor noticed that one end of the porch had a ramp, so someone in the household must have a need for the ramp.

John Fargo walked with a slight limp, and his facial features were those of a typical rancher, with a well-tanned, weathered, and wrinkled face. He stood about six foot and two inches and had a deep sounding tone to his voice. John Fargo said, "I assume you are here to talk about the part time work I mentioned."

"That is correct, sir," Trevor replied. "They felt I was lacking experience at the Skyline Ranch, so I thought I would check with you on the part time work you mentioned."

"Well son, it's mostly shoveling horse manure in the barn and some of the surrounding area. There is a small room in the loft that you can stay in, with a shower and microwave. You do have the option to raid the kitchen in the main house, and meals will be included providing you are on time. Does this sound like anything you would be interested in? Do you have any questions?"

"Yes, I am interested," replied Trevor. The only question Trevor could come up with was: "I assume I can ride the horses in my free time?"

"That would be correct, but first check with me as some of the horses can be difficult and I do not want you getting hurt."

Chapter 2

Susan gathered the blanket that was covering her lap, exposing the wheelchair she was sitting in, and proceeded to wheel herself to the screened front door. Trevor noted that she was rather good looking, with a fine shape for her seventeen years. Her brown hair was pulled tightly into a ponytail and, if she could smile, she was keeping it a secret. She had nothing to say as she passed by Trevor on her way to the door. John Fargo took the opportunity to inform Trevor that he was to keep his distance from his daughter and to always be concerned about her safety whenever she was in the barn area.

"She had a horse accident two years ago and has not had a successful recovery. You will find she pretty much stays to herself and is not much of a talker."

Trevor said he understood and would do his best to look out for her when she was in the barn.

John Fargo said it was not likely Susan would be in the barn very much, as "she is a little afraid of horses since the accident. Work starts at daylight, so I will see you at breakfast, if you make it on time. My wife, Lilly, is in town at some church function, so try not to scare her to death in the morning."

Trevor unloaded his backpack and located his phone. He made a call to Candy Wade, who was his go to gal whenever he needed help. She was twenty-one-years-old and still going to school. When Trevor needed to learn how to kiss a girl, she answered an ad he had posted in a local newspaper—she turned out to be an excellent teacher. Ever since, whenever Trevor needed help with anything, he called Candy.

Trevor explained his new job, and told her he need-ed some clothes, boots, and a cowboy hat delivered to the Running Water Ranch by noon the next day. She said she was on it, and she would be there before noon. She had all the pertinent sizes as she had been taking care of him since he had placed his initial ad. He felt he had probably provided most of her income for her schooling, as he paid her well for dropping everything and taking care of the little projects he came up with.

The lights were on in the house when Trevor looked out the window in the loft. Candy would not be at the ranch until noon, so Trevor just put on what he had worn the day before and hoped he would not ruin anything before Candy's arrival.

When Trevor entered the house, Lilly Fargo was busy in the kitchen. She saw him come in and introduced herself as Lilly and told Trevor to take a seat at the kitchen table. "Breakfast is just about ready. How do you like your eggs?"

"Any way is fine," Trevor replied.

"Good, because that is how you are going to get them," she said with a big smile on her face. "You're a little overdressed for barn work."

"My clothes will be arriving about noon, as I did not bring any extra with me," was Trevor's reply.

"Well just take a look in the box on the front porch and you will probably find some rubber boots and an old coat that will do until your stuff arrives."

John Fargo entered the kitchen and they began eating. They had just finished eating when Susan arrived in her wheelchair. Lilly was surprised to see Susan up so early in the morning—she was normally not an early riser during the summer break.

John said, "Let's go and I'll show you what you need to do first thing every morning."

They went to the barn and turned out the horses. John then pointed out that the stalls needed to be mucked out and fresh hay scattered about. "You want to make sure the watering troughs outside are full, so the horses have plenty of water. Next, take a look out in the front yard to make sure there are no piles of manure from the cows or horses that might have found their way into the yard—they get out there on occasion and I get yelled at by Lilly if she steps in anything. This should last you until noon and then you have the rest of the day off, unless I have some special project."

Trevor was about halfway done with mucking out the stalls when Susan came rolling her wheelchair into the barn. Trevor immediately looked for cow pies that he may have missed, but the runway looked clear. Trevor said, "Good morning," and Susan pointed out that she was getting some feed for the chickens. She said her job was to feed the chickens and gather eggs. She wanted to know if Trevor had cleaned out the chicken coup runway. He replied that he had not been told to do so, but if she would show him where it was, he would do it right away.

Trevor asked if he could help get the feed for the chickens. Susan replied "No," and stated she was not helpless. Trevor was startled by the tone in her voice but let it pass. As they approached the chicken coup it was obvious that someone had already cleaned out the walkway in the coup so Trevor said he would return to the barn. John must have cleaned out the chicken coup before he went on to other chores.

As Trevor was cleaning out the last stall, Susan returned to the barn and stopped by the stall Trevor was cleaning. She did take a moment to look him over a little as she had not given any thought to the fact that he was quite good-looking. She seemed as though she was having trouble gathering her thoughts and trying to figure out what she wanted to say to Trevor. She finally said, "I know we do not know each other very well, but I was wondering if you could help me with a project I want to try and accomplish?"

She proceeded, with a great deal of effort, to stand up out of her wheelchair. By holding on to the top rail in the stall, she managed to stand by herself. Trevor was not sure what to do as he had been instructed to make sure she did not get hurt in the barn.

As Susan supported herself on the top of the stall, you could see that her strength was beginning to fade. Susan explained that the doctors had said there was nothing physically wrong with her, and the fact she could not walk was more mental than physical. She proceeded to slip slowly back into her chair.

"There is a dance just before school starts and I want to be able to dance with my father before the start of the next school year. I wanted to know if you would help me. I know I can be a little difficult at times, but I will try to control my temper and my mouth. I know I need to get physically stronger, and I have a plan. I want to stand at the first stall and eventually work my way to the second and finally the sixth as my first goal, without the aid of the wheelchair. I can't let my parents help as they just make me nervous, and they worry about me falling. I want this to be a surprise for my dad; we will need to keep this between the two of us. I know this will be difficult, so I will need to find some incentive to keep me working toward my first goal." Trevor did not mean to blurt out his first thought, but said: "How about a kiss after each goal is achieved?" Trevor embarrassed himself by having voiced his thoughts and it also embarrassed Susan, as she had never been kissed by a boy.

"Let me think about that, as it must be a goal that will keep me going. I normally have difficulty talking to anyone, as I am self-conscious about my wheelchair; but you make it easy to talk with you because you listen. Let's start in the morning."

"Sounds good to me," Trevor said. "But we need to make sure you don't get hurt." He noticed that she had not answered his suggestion about the kiss.

The next day as Lilly was cooking breakfast Trevor came into the kitchen. The aroma of the bacon and eggs filled the air and Trevor was starving. She asked if he would like a cup of coffee and he said that would be great.

Susan entered the room dressed as though she was intending to go to the barn. Again, Lilly was surprised that Susan would be up this early. "What's going on?" Lilly asked.

"I am going to go out and keep Trevor company in the barn."

Lilly had suspected that Trevor had something to do with Susan getting up early, but she was not aware that Susan had any interest in Trevor. After the kids had left for the barn, John came into the kitchen and asked Lilly if he had heard Susan's voice. She told him Susan was going out to keep Trevor company in the barn.

"Don't ask me," Lilly said. "I don't know what is going on, but I will keep my eye on the two of them."

As Trevor entered the barn, he said he would clean stall number one once all the horses were turned out. Susan wheeled her chair over to the front of the stall and began the process of getting out of her chair, while clinging to the top of the stall. She did manage to get up and drag herself to the end of stall number two. She asked Trevor to get her wheelchair, as she was totally exhausted. She fell to the ground before Trevor could get to her with the wheelchair and she banged her chin on the bottom board of the stall. She was a bit woozy, so Trevor picked her up and liked feeling her body against his.

He heard her say, "You going to hold me all day or put me in my chair?" He replied that he would not mind holding her all day. Her cheeks turned pink as Trevor had embarrassed her and she said, "Put me in my chair, please." She could feel his strength and how easily he had lifted her off the ground.

Trevor reminded her it was going to be a process, so not to get into a rush. They heard the screen door on the house slam—someone was coming. Trevor handed Susan a rag to wipe her face and turned her chair so that her scraped chin would not be visible to anyone coming into the barn.

John stuck his head into the barn to tell Trevor that he was going to drive into town to pick up some supplies. Trevor said, "Fine," and Susan said, "Goodbye, Dad."

Trevor told Susan: "You are going to have to figure out a story about your chin as it is going to be quite visible." Trevor finished up his mucking out of the stalls and made sure the water troughs were full.

"I am done for the day," he said. "What would you like to do?" he asked Susan. She tried standing one more time and then said, "I want to see if my legs are strong enough to ride a horse."

"Wow," said Trevor. "Where did that come from? You trying to get me killed by your dad?"

"I just want you to help me get onto a horse and lead me around inside the corral to see if I have enough strength in my legs to give commands to a horse—I promise I won't do anything stupid."

"Your mom and dad would kill me if I put you on a horse, and you know it."

Susan said, "Let's use the corral in the back of the barn so Mom cannot see us. We can use Morning Star, as she is the smallest and oldest horse we have."

"Are you sure you want to do this?" Trevor asked again.

After getting Morning Star all tacked up and into the back corral, Trevor found the three-step box that was used to help older people get onto horses. He put Susan's chair next to the side of the corral and then lifted her into his arms and carried her to the step box. After climbing up the steps, it was easy to get Susan into the saddle. He told her to stay put until he moved the box to the edge of the corral. Of course, Susan did not listen and had Morning Star on the move.

"Look Trevor, I can do it—I have enough strength to signal Morning Star what I want her to do."

"Show me you can go into a trot and then a canter," Trevor said. Trevor had been reading up on horses, so he was aware of typical terms associated with horse movements. Susan did as instructed and the horse performed as requested.

"Are you getting any support from your legs to keep you from falling from the saddle?" Trevor asked. Susan said she was getting enough to keep herself from falling. "Please go saddle Smoke, so we can go for a short ride in the pasture," she said.

Trevor was not sure what he was doing. He had only tacked a horse a few times and only ridden for perhaps a total of four hours—he knew this was not a good idea. Trevor tacked up Smoke and they left the corral. "Let's ride into the pasture adjacent to the road as I want to feel the wind in my hair."

"No galloping, Susan," said Trevor. "If you fall, I will get fired."

They had ridden to the far end of the pasture and were starting back toward the barn when Susan's dad could be seen driving down the road toward the ranch. Trevor knew that he would be very angry. John was not sure what to say when he realized it was Susan on Morning Star.

As they all converged on the house, Lilly had also seen what was happening and rushed out onto the front porch and straight to John's truck. She opened his door and told him to bite his tongue. She said, "We can talk about this later. This is a good thing, and we should be happy about what is happening. We might just get our girl back if we leave them alone—somehow, they have developed a connection, and she is letting Trevor help her."

Trevor dismounted at the front of the barn and led the two horses to the back of the barn where he helped Susan down from the horse and onto a bale of hay. Once in her chair, she thanked Trevor. "Trevor, I loved that. I had better go face the music as I am sure someone is going to be mad at me or maybe you," she said with a grin.

As Susan approached her mom and dad on the porch of the house, she did not understand why no one was yelling at her. Lilly gave her a big hug and said, "I am so proud of you."

"Dad, we tried it out in the corral first to make sure my legs were strong enough to signal the horse and they worked fine. Don't blame Trevor as I talked him into it," Susan said.

"What happened to your chin?" her dad asked.

"I was trying to stand by a stall, and I slipped and fell. Trevor picked me up and put me back into my chair."

Trevor had decided it was best to hide out in the back of the barn, as he was sure John was not a happy camper regarding their horse-riding episode.

Susan went to the house to clean up for dinner and John proceeded to the barn to have a few words with Trevor. As soon as he saw Trevor, he said, "I thought I told you to be sure my daughter does not get hurt in the barn. How are you doing on that?" Then he turned and walked back to the house.

Dinner was a little quieter than normal, other than Susan talking about how great it was to ride Morning Star. After dinner, Susan came out to the barn to see if her dad had yelled at Trevor.

"Everything is fine," Trevor said, even though he assumed he was on probation. Trevor finished his night's work and Susan again made it to stall number two before needing help to her chair. She thanked Trevor for the wonderful day and gave a shy grin as she headed back toward the house.

Susan made a great effort for the rest of the week and managed to get to stall five. She was also doing exercises in her bedroom, which had previously been recommended by her doctor. There was a definite improvement in her leg strength—Trevor was sure she would make it to stall six within the next couple of days.

Trevor was spending as much time on Smoke as possible and was starting to see an improvement in his horseback riding whenever possible Susan would go with him and give advice so that he would quit bouncing in his saddle.

Susan still had not said anything about the reward she was expecting when she accomplished her goal. She had fallen three times during the week, but she would not give up. Her parents had not said anything about the bruises on her forearms, although Susan had been wearing longer-sleeved shirts, attempting to hide them as much as possible.

Lilly had definitely noticed a major change in Susan's attitude and personality since Trevor had arrived. She had really come out of her shell and was seeming to be more like her old self.

Next morning, Susan was on time for breakfast and was sure this was going to be the day. She could not wait to get to the barn. As Trevor began turning out the horses, Susan was already to stall three. She took a short breath and then made it to stall five. Her energy level was still good, and she proceeded to stall six. "Yes," she said. "Yes!" She asked Trevor to get her wheelchair. As Trevor got her to her chair and prior to sitting down, she said it was time for him to pay up. At first Trevor did not understand, but as she slipped her arms around his neck, he understood. He pulled her closer to his chest and gave her a big kiss. All she remembered was his warm lips touching hers and how secure she felt in his arms. He was holding her so tight that she did not need legs to stand—she thought she was floating on a cloud. She could feel his hold beginning to loosen and realized she was going to have to sit in her chair. She thanked him and began to wheel herself back toward the house. She stopped for a moment and asked Trevor what the second goal would be. He replied, "You need to walk to stall six with no support."

"I can hardly wait," she said with a shy grin crossing her face.

Chapter 3

As Trevor was going toward the house for lunch, he thought about the kiss and realized it was also a reward for him. He had found it quite enjoyable and would like it to happen again. He also realized it could not happen again until Susan met her second goal, or she might not work hard enough to reach it. He had to remember—no free kisses unless she earned them.

Lilly had made them sandwiches for lunch. Susan pointed out to Trevor that the next reward would be one kiss and driving lessons in the pasture or on the road to the ranch, as the new goal would require more effort than the first. Trevor said, "Well, we will see," with a grin on his face. Susan playfully slapped his arm, knowing he was only teasing her. Trevor wondered how he was going to teach her as he did not even know how to drive.

As the week progressed, Susan was making great progress as her leg strength was really beginning to show. They had even taken the horses on a couple of long trail rides during the week.

On Friday, Susan wanted Trevor to walk by her side, as she was going to try for six stalls. Her last four steps were a little wobbly, but she made it, remembering that she was working for a kiss. Trevor caught her before she fell and carried her to her wheelchair.

She said, "OK, time to pay up." Trevor played as if he was not sure what she meant, but she placed her arms around his neck to make sure he knew what was expected. He placed his hands in the small of her back and drew her toward him as their lips touched. She ran her fingers through the hair on the back of his head and definitely returned his kiss as he drew his hands up toward the middle of her back, pulling her tighter and tighter. He was holding her as tight as possible, and it seemed as though the kiss would never end.

Trevor said, "We need to stay focused on your dance goal." He pulled her close again and gave her a peck on the cheek. He placed her in her wheelchair and said, "Next week, we walk down the six stalls and then across the walkway to the other side of the barn." She smiled that shy grin and said, "That is really going to be hard—I wonder what the reward for that should be?" Trevor ignored her grin and said, "We will also start to practice some dance steps to prepare you for the dance. I will find a pickup tomorrow so we can start our driving lessons."

"I will see you at the house for lunch," Susan said. "But first—one more kiss." Trevor bent over and gave her a peck on the cheek and said, "I will see you soon."

At lunch, Lilly could feel that there was something going on between Susan and Trevor. "Why are you two so smiley today?"

"Trevor is going to take me to the 'before school dance.' Isn't that exciting?" Susan said.

Lilly said, "Well, we had better do some shopping for a dress and shoes."

"Don't need to, Mom. Trevor called Candy Wade and she is taking care of everything. Come on Trevor, let's go for a trail ride."

"Give me about an hour," Trevor said. "As I have a couple things I need to do."

Trevor phoned Candy Wade and told her what type of truck he wanted delivered to the ranch on Saturday at about noon, as John and Lilly were planning on going to town. He also asked her to pick him up for driving lessons in the truck on Friday. He said he would make up an excuse to Susan to explain leaving the ranch.

After Trevor had left, Lilly said, "OK, what's going on with you two?" Susan just could not keep quiet a minute longer. "Mom, Trever kissed me." Lilly said, "Really. What did you think about that?"

"I really like him a lot, Mom. He's helping me with a project I am working on, and we just sort of grew closer to one another. I think I am more than fond of him, but he said we would talk about it more after the dance."

"Susan, I think it's okay to like a young man, but you are so young. I don't think you know what a real relationship is, but we can talk more about this feeling you're having after the dance. What's this project you are working on?"

"You'll just have to wait and see," said Susan.

Friday rolled around and Trevor told Susan that he had some business to take care of, and Candy was picking him up about ten a.m. Susan said "OK," and did not make a big deal about it.

Candy arrived and told Trevor they just had to go about five miles down the road and they would be at the property where they would have their driving lessons. The pickup was just perfect—it was a 1951 Chevrolet with dents on both doors and one back fender. It had a standard six-cylinder motor with a three-speed shift on the column. Candy pointed out the brake pedal and emergency brake first, as she said these were the most important features for a beginner to know. Then came the clutch and gas pedal. She explained how the shifter worked and how to back up. "Ready, let's go," Candy said.

Trevor killed the motor the first two times he tried to go forward. It's not as easy as it looks, he thought to himself. Candy kept saying to let the clutch out slower.

Finally, they started moving forward in the field they were practicing in. After bouncing around for a couple hours, Trevor was getting the hang of it and told Candy that he thought that he had enough practice for the day.

She said, "One more lesson." She had him drive to the road along the edge of the field and said, "Let's see if you can drive down this road and back without going into the ditch."

Trevor took off down the road and Candy kept yelling: "Slow down or you're going to miss the corner!" Sure enough, they missed the corner and went into the ditch with a bang and suddenly stopped.

"Are you alright, Candy?" Her head had hit the dash, and she was bleeding slightly on her forehead. She said she was okay. Trevor raced around the truck and helped her get out on her side. "I am so sorry," he said as he held her in his arms. She was a little shaken up and it felt comforting to be held. Finally, she said, "Let's see if we can back this truck out of the ditch and get it back on the road."

"I will put it in reverse, and you push from the front."

Slowly the pickup began to move back and on to the road. "Get in," she said. "I will drive us back to the car. I do not think there is any damage to the truck so I will have it delivered on schedule tomorrow."

Trevor said, "I am not sure you could damage this piece of junk. I am sorry about the bump on your forehead—we will go to the hospital and get it checked out just to be sure you don't have a concussion."

Chapter 4

The next day, John and Lilly were off to town early in the morning, as expected. Candy had the pickup delivered at noon, right on schedule. The delivery truck unloaded the pickup in the field, next to the road to the ranch.

Trevor helped Susan walk to the pickup, leaving her wheelchair next to the gate entrance. Trevor pointed out the pedals and explained how the shifter worked. Susan had a little experience driving on the ranch before her accident, so she was ready to go. She started the truck and killed the motor the first time, but finally it was moving forward on the second attempt. What had looked like a nice smooth field was exceptionally bouncy in the pickup. It was a good thing Susan had been doing her leg exercises, as it allowed her to work the clutch and brakes with ease.

After about a half hour, Trevor said, "It's my turn." Susan was reluctant to give up as she was having so much fun, so she said, "All right, but only for fifteen minutes."

Trevor did fine and soon Susan said it was her turn—this time she wanted to drive up the two-mile dirt driveway and back to the ranch house. Trevor told her about his wreck, pointing out that it was not as easy as it looked. He wanted her to be careful, so he did not get in trouble with her dad. They had not shifted out of first gear so far and they would probably do this on the way up the driveway.

Susan did fine going up the road then stopped and turned around at the end of the road. She had ground the gears on the shift to second gear, but Trevor had done the same the day before.

As they headed back toward the ranch, the unexpected happened—John and Lilly had turned onto the road to the ranch and saw the pickup ahead sort of weaving around as it went down the road. Trevor and Susan had seen her mom and dad turn in behind them. Trevor said, "Go slow, Susan, and do not wreck. Don't be nervous. Your dad is going to kill me—I guess I am the one that should be nervous."

John was trying to figure out why this pickup was weaving a little and going rather slow. "You've got to be shitting me," as he finally realized what was going on. Lilly asked what the problem was. "That is Susan and Trevor in that truck. I am going to kill him," was all that John could say.

Lilly said, "Now bite your lip, John. This is a good thing, and I don't think you should say anything. This is all helping Susan come back to us."

"I'm going to kill him; I swear," was John's reply. "Slow down so you don't make them nervous. We don't want to cause a wreck."

As Trevor and Susan approached the open gate to the field, Susan pulled into the field and kept going. She had forgotten they were still in second gear and almost hit the gate post. They were really bouncing hard this time, as they were still in second gear and going faster than their first practice, so she braked and killed the engine. "What a blast!" she yelled. She restarted the pickup and headed toward the gate where her mom and dad were waiting. She was laughing her head off all the way, but finally realized the fun was about to end. Susan almost forgot about her legs and was about to jump out of the pickup when Trevor yelled: "Stop! Remember, I need to give you a piggyback ride to your wheelchair."

It was about forty yards to the gate and Susan was laughing her head off, pretending to shift gears and using Trevor's nose as a shifter. John had to turn away to keep from laughing. All you could hear him say was, "Dam it."

"Oh Mom, I have never had so much fun.," Susan said.

"Well, you go on to the house dear, and Dad and I will have a little talk with Trevor."

"I don't even know what to say," was all John could say as he turned and walked toward the house.

"Trevor, what in the hell is the matter with you," Lilly said. "We expect you to take care of Susan when we leave her with you, and what do you do but go driving in a piece of shit truck when neither of you know how to drive." Trevor offered no response and Lilly just shook her head as she headed toward the ranch house.

Trevor decided to skip dinner, as he felt it would not be comfortable around the table. Susan could not stop talking as she was so excited about her day. Susan fixed Trevor a plate and said she was going to take it to the barn. John wanted to say something but bit his tongue. He looked at Lilly and said, "What are we going to do about those two? We can't ground her, as she doesn't go anywhere, and we can't spank her because she is too old. I swear, I don't know what to do, but I will have a few words with Mr. Tremaine tomorrow. I know it's like pouring water on a duck's back, but I have to say something. He just does not understand."

"Don't worry John, it will work itself out. Did you see how happy she was? This is not the same girl that lived here before Trevor came to work for us. Oh, by the way John, Trevor's birthday is next Wednesday. Other than shooting him, what do you think we should do?"

Susan rolled into the barn and yelled for Trevor, who emerged from the back of the barn. "I brought you some food."

"Thank you, I am starving," said Trevor. "How was dinner?"

"A little quieter," she said.

"I can hardly wait until tomorrow," Trevor said.

"What is my reward going to be for the next goal?" Susan asked. "You know I walk and dance good enough now to dance with my dad."

"Don't worry," Trevor said. "I've got that covered and I will tell you when you achieve the next goal." Susan left for the house, wondering what Trevor had in mind.

Chapter 5

Summer had sped by and soon it was one week before the dance. Trevor had bought a motorcycle right after his eighteenth birthday, and a ride was one of Susan's rewards, along with a kiss—that was followed by a helicopter ride, a boogie board ride behind a ski boat, a hot air balloon ride, and other outdoor events that Susan could participate in without raising suspicions about her legs with her mom and dad.

John had managed to survive without having a heart attack. Lilly was concerned about how close Trevor and Susan had become. Susan was now ninety percent recovered and could walk a mile, and Trevor had no concerns about her being able to dance three or four consecutive dances in a row. Everything seemed ready for the big dance.

Candy Wade made it in late on the Friday night before the dance and contacted Susan to tell her they were having a spa day on Saturday morning. She said she would deliver Susan to the dance in time for the first dance; Trevor was to meet them there.

Susan had never really had a spa day, so she was counting on Candy to show her the ropes. It all began by spending some time in the sauna and then a massage; this was followed by lunch and then a pedicure and manicure. Last was the hair, which was pulled up in the back and deposited in a tight bun on the top of her head. Makeup was applied, and then Candy helped her get dressed in the gown she had ordered from New York City.

Candy said, "You are about ready to go—all we need are some flowers for you to give to your parents."

As Susan looked in the mirror, she did not recognize the person looking back at her. "Oh Candy, thank you so much. I look so different, and a bit more grown up."

Candy said, "You look beautiful. I am sure you will be the prettiest girl at the dance. I also bought Trevor's outfit and you two will be the best dressed couple at the dance. There has been a slight change in plans, as the dance tradition is to always start with a waltz— that means you and Trevor will need to dance first, and the second dance will be with your father. Let's get into the limousine before we are late."

As they approached the dance hall at the fair-grounds, Trevor could see the limo pulling up behind the stage. As Susan stepped from the limo all Trevor could say was: "Absolutely beautiful. You are stunning."

Susan blushed a little and she could hear the stage manager announcing the first dance would be a Viennese waltz, as was the tradition. "Let's get this show on the road," Susan said. Trevor had to repeat himself by telling Susan she was stunningly beautiful. Susan said, "Thank you." She felt beautiful.

John and Lilly were seated about one row back in the table seating and had an excellent view of the dance floor.

As the music started, this young couple walked up to the dance floor, on the opposite side of John and Lilly. As other couples were starting to dance, Trevor and Susan began to move about the floor. They stood out in their beautiful clothing, as they glided through the various steps in perfect harmony with one another. Many couples had stopped talking to admire the couple dancing so beautifully about the floor.

"Oh my God," Lilly said, as she dropped her drink in the middle of the table. John rushed to her side and with a concerned voice asked, "What's the matter?" Tears began to flow from Lilly's eyes as she pointed at the dance floor and said, "That's Trevor and Susan dancing to the waltz." John's eyes also begin to tear up seeing his beautiful daughter floating around the dance floor.

As the dance ended, Susan said thank you to Trevor, and said, "It's time to pay up."

"You mean right here?" he asked. And as her arms slipped around his neck, he gave her the long-awaited reward.

The whole audience clapped, many not yet realizing it was Susan Fargo, the "crippled girl," that they were looking at. The announcer then requested that Mr. John Fargo come to the dance floor, as his daughter had requested the next dance with him. It was then that everyone knew what was happening and then total clapping, hollering, and whistling almost drowned out the music.

When the dance was over, John and Susan returned to where Lilly and Trevor were sitting. John thanked Susan for the dance he'd thought he would never have, tears still filling his eyes.

Susan looked at Trevor and said, "Time to pay up." Trevor said "All right, as he took her into his arms, held her as tight as he could, and gave her the final reward for the long journey they had taken. After the kiss Susan said, "I might need my wheelchair again after a kiss like that." Lilly said, "Well if you don't, I might."

The rest of Susan's night was filled dancing with Trevor and a few other young men who ask Susan to dance. In between dances, they were trying to tell the story to Susan's parents, about how the whole thing came about from start to finish. Susan's parents just could not believe what the kids had accomplished.

Chapter 6

A week had passed and Susan was still the talk of the local community. The story of what had happened was being shared by Lilly and everyone in the county was astonished by what had been accomplished.

Later that night at dinnertime, Susan got a phone call from Stan Blackfield, who was the captain and quarterback of the high school football team. He was probably the most popular boy in school. He wanted to know if Susan would like to go to a movie matinee this coming Sunday. She had answered the call in the living room, so no one had heard her say that yes, she would like to go. She could not believe that Stan Blackfield had asked her to go to a show. Susan loved Trevor and to her this was no more than going to the show with a friend; she saw no reason to involve Trevor.

After dinner, she told Lilly about the invitation. Lilly wanted to know what Trevor thought about the date, which she had agreed to with Stan. "I have not told him," Was Susan's reply. "It's not a date, it's just going to a show."

"Well," Lilly said. "What would you call it?" Susan got a little flustered as she was not quite sure what to say, so she said she would talk to Trevor about it.

Susan went to the barn to tell Trevor about the show. Trevor was obviously upset and a little hurt, but he tried not to let it show. "It's not a date, Trevor—it's just like going to the afternoon show with a friend."

"How long have you known this friend?" Trevor wanted to know. Trevor had never heard Stan's name mentioned before.

"He is a new friend," was Susan's reply, as she turned and headed to the house.

On Sunday, Stan showed up by midmorning in his fancy new truck and escorted Susan from the house to his truck, opening the door for her to get in. As they drove toward the movie theater, Susan felt a little awkward as she had not been with anyone but Trevor for a long time.

Trevor had gone to John to ask if he could work in the high pasture for a while. There was a small bunkhouse holding up to four people, and ranch hands usually stayed there for three to four weeks before returning to the ranch. The good part was that all they did was round up wild mustangs and break them right there in the corral adjacent to the bunkhouse. Trevor just felt he needed some space from Susan, and this was far enough away she would not come to see him by herself.

John made the arrangements and sent Trevor on his way before Susan had returned from the show. Stan had attempted to put his arm around Susan a couple times during the show, but she managed to squirm around enough to let him know the attempts were not welcome. When they got home from the show, Susan thanked Stan and avoided any attempt at a kiss by letting herself out of the pickup and heading straight for the house. Lilly was inside and asked how her date had gone. Susan reminded her it was not a date and said she was a little uncomfortable, but the show was all right. Susan was very naïve in believing this had not been a date.

Susan said she was going to the barn to tell Trevor about the show and how she had avoided Stan's attempts to put his arm around her. Lilly said, "Trevor is not in the barn."

"Where is he?" Susan asked.

"Your dad sent him to the high pasture to help with the wild mustangs."

Why would he do that, Susan wondered, as she headed outside to find her dad. The harder she looked for her dad, the madder she got. Finally, she found him out by the chicken coop fixing some fencing. "Why did you send Trevor to the high pasture? I will not be able to have him help me with some projects we have been talking about." John could tell she was fighting mad by the tone in her voice. "Just a minute, young lady. In the first place, Trevor came to me and asked to work up there—it was not my idea. When I asked why, he told me he wanted to learn how to ride wild horses. We both knew he was going to learn the hard way, but he said that was what he wanted to do. He's going to get a few bruises and hopefully no broken bones."

Susan went storming toward the house to talk with her mom. "Mom, Dad says Trevor asked to go to the high pasture. Why would he do that?"

Lilly said, "I told you he was not going to like you going out on that date with Stan. I guess he is just giving you some room to figure it out."

"Figure what out?" Susan said. "I just went to an afternoon show."

Trevor had arrived in the high pasture and two other ranch hands were working with the horses. They were both skinny looking, but you could tell they were all muscle, as the work they did was extremely hard. Thomas Jones walked with a slight limp, probably from being thrown from a horse too many times. Johnny Carr was tough as nails, with a cowboy hat that was totally round. It looked different when you were use to seeing formed cowboy hats.

Trevor shook hands and could tell he would need to improve his strength, as both Johnny and Thomas had an extremely strong grip. Trevor told them right up front that he was just learning to ride broncs so not to spare him because he was a rookie—just tell him what to do and turn him loose.

Johnny asked Trevor why John would send him up to the north pasture if he had no experience riding broncs. "I asked to come," said Trevor. "I needed some time to work out a couple of issues and I figured this would be a good place to do it." No more questions were asked.

The next day they started by rounding up ten mustangs and corralling them next to the bunkhouse. Johnny described how Trevor should go about riding the horse and then let Trevor go. Trevor spent most of the day on the ground while learning the trade. He did manage to get two of the horses broken, but the goal for the day was five. Johnny said they would help the next day, but Trevor said no, he was all right and wanted to continue—even though he could barely walk to the bunkhouse, he repeated that he wanted to ride again tomorrow.

Trevor could not understand how Susan could go out with someone else after all they had gone through. His anger would not subside. The more he thought about it, the madder he got.

The next morning, after breakfast, they were at it again. This time Trevor did much better, but only because his anger would not let him be thrown from the horses. Johnny told Thomas, "That young man has some serious issues. I saw some tears coming from his eyes as he rode some of those horses. Someone has hurt him very bad, and I am not sure taking it out on the horses is going to help him."

Thomas said, "Let's take a day off tomorrow to let Trevor's body recover and enjoy the country; that might help the young man."

It had been four weeks since Trevor had gone to the high pasture and Susan was getting anxious for his return, as she was missing him dearly. On Tuesday night, Stan Blackfield called for Susan. Susan answered the phone and Stan wanted to know if she would be interested in going to the Friday night football game, followed by the school dance. Susan had never been asked to a football ballgame and although she knew Trevor might be a little upset, she told Stan that she would go with him as a friend.

Her judgement was again clouded by the excitement of being asked to the ballgame by the most popular boy in school. She knew in her heart that this was a poor decision. She was not sure when Trevor would return to the ranch. She rationalized that going to a ballgame and dancing with a friend could not cause any harm. Again, she did not consider Trevor's feelings.

When Friday arrived, Trevor had finally gotten back from the high pasture. Susan ran up to greet him when she saw him go into the barn. "I missed you so much," she said. She gave him a big hug and kiss, then continued to squeeze him as hard as she could.

"How about dinner in town tonight?" Trevor asked, as they had not seen each other for the four weeks he was gone. Susan thought for a moment and then said she could not go as she had already made plans to go to the high school football game.

"Would you like me to go with you?" Trevor asked. "No, I am going with Stan as he called earlier in the week and ask me to go." All Trevor said was: "Well, all right then; maybe some other time." He proceeded to the loft to get cleaned up from being out in the high pasture so long. The tears rolling down his face spoke to the true feelings his heart was having. He felt he and Susan were broken, and he did not know how to fix it.

Susan went to the house and told her mom what had happened and said she was not sure how Trevor felt about the date with Stan. "You know I love Trevor; I just keep making these stupid decisions."

"It's called growing up," Lilly said.

Later, Trevor walked up to the house to talk with John just as Stan arrived to pick up Susan. It was awkward at the door and Susan felt so bad as she walked away, with Stan holding her hand all the way to the truck.

John came into the room and asked Trevor how things had gone in the high pasture. He had already gotten a full report from Thomas but wanted Trevor's opinion of how he had done. Trevor said he had learned a lot and felt he now knew how to ride and break a wild horse. His herding and roping were greatly improved, but still needed more work. Trevor said the reason he had come to the house was to let John know he would be leaving the Running Water Ranch, as it was time to move on.

Lilly had heard the discussion and told Trevor that she knew Susan loved Trevor and she was sure that Trevor also loved Susan. "You are correct, Mrs. Lilly, but we both have a lot of growing up to do before we can even think about getting more serious. Susan has a lot to learn about life, as do I. I think it's just better for me to leave now."

John said, "I hate to see you go, but remember you are always welcome back at the ranch."

Trevor said, "Thank you. I will have Candy arrange to have my stuff picked up. I am leaving on my motorcycle."

With that he left the house, picked up the backpack by his bike, and headed down the road for the Cheyenne Rodeo.

When Susan arrived home, she was walked to the door by Stan, and she allowed him to kiss her goodnight. It was more a mechanical kiss and nothing like when Trevor kissed her. She then went immediately into the house, as she needed Stan to leave so she could go talk to Trevor. She told Lilly that she had a good time at the game and dance but felt bad about Trevor all the time she was there. "Then I let Stan kiss me good night at the door. What should I do? I feel I need to tell Trevor I am sorry about everything. I am going to go to the barn to see Trevor."

Lilly said, "He's not there, Susan. He came to the house to tell Dad and me he was leaving, and then he got on his motorcycle and left."

"When is he coming back?" Susan asked.

"I don't think he will be coming back," was Lilly's reply. Tears began to form in Susan's eyes. "You mean he has left for good?"

"I think that's correct," Lilly replied, as Susan's tears began to flow like a waterfall.

"No Mom, that cannot be true—I love Trevor and he loves me."

"Well, my dear you have a funny way of showing it. I think you broke Trevor's heart, and he now needs to move on as do you. Trying to wish him back will not work," Lilly said.

"But all of his stuff is here; he could not have taken it with him on his bike."

"He will send Candy to pick it up in a few days," was Lilly's reply.

Susan went to her room and cried until she finally fell asleep. Her heart had also been broken—a love so deep and true had been broken.

Chapter 7

When Trevor arrived at the rodeo grounds in Cheyenne, the place was bustling with activity. He first went to the man in charge of the stockyard and yes, they needed a hand with shoveling manure, moving fencing, and exercising horses. The pay was minimal, but they did provide a small seventeen-foot trailer to sleep in. Trevor took the job.

He was told to report to Jessie Slocomb in the barn area, and she would tell him what to do. Trevor just had to keep busy to keep Susan out of his thoughts. Jessie was about twenty-six and had stunning bright red hair. Trevor introduced himself and said he was reporting for duty. Jessie looked him over and thought he was a little young for this type of work—usually, they sent her older, down on their luck alcoholics or homeless individuals looking to make a few bucks. Then they would quit, leaving her to try and figure out how to get the job done and keep the place running on schedule. "Work starts at five a.m., and you are off at noon. Sound, all right?" Trevor asked where he was to start. "Go to the far end of the barn and work your way to the other end. You probably won't get it all done on your shift, so someone else will come in and finish the rest." She turned and walked away, headed for her next project. Trevor did notice that she did justice to those tight-fitting jeans she was wearing.

Shoveling manure was not exactly his lifelong ambition, but it was part of his goal to work hard and see if he could get any satisfaction out of the work. To Jessie's amazement, Trevor had almost completed cleaning the whole barn when she returned to show his replacement his chores. Trevor asked where he needed to go to sign up for the bronc riding rodeo event. She gave him directions and this time it was her turn to notice how good he looked in his tight-fitting jeans. She thought to herself that this kid was a real keeper for someone, as he obviously knew how to work and was very pleasant on the eyes. Even though he was younger than her, it never hurts to window shop.

Trevor had just signed up for the bronc and bull riding events when a young lady, about his age, asked if he could ride a horse. Trevor said he could probably give it a try, with a wide grin running from one end of his face to the other. "Can you rope a steer very good?" she asked. Trevor gave himself an average, in that as he had only roped wild horses. She said her name was Lou

Hensley, and she needed a partner in the team roping event. "Well, you're going to have to do. I am out of time for signing up and my partner is not here. Come on, let's get signed up—we are up in half an hour. This is what I want you to do: When the gate opens, I want you to throw your rope on the count of three. Just guess where you think his head is going to be and throw. I will do the same for the feet. We probably won't connect at either end but that is what I want you to do. Got it?"

Trevor said, "All right, let's go. You got us a couple of horses?"

"That's taken care of, let's go." Said Lou.

Trevor and Lou were both in the arena with the steer in the chute. The gate opened and the steer took off. Trevor was counting: one, two, three—and he threw the rope where he thought the head of the steer would be and to his surprise, he guessed correctly. His rope tightened around the steer's neck. Lou also guessed correctly, and they were ahead on the leader board. "You just got yourself a buckle, cowboy," was all Lou said. "No one's going to beat that time."

Trevor headed for the bronc riding event, as it was next. He was first up and had drawn a horse named Broken Heart. He thought to himself, well, that was appropriate. Broken Heart had never been ridden for the full eight seconds before, and a couple of riders had passed on him, which allowed Trevor to pull his name. Trevor knew this was going to be a difficult ride.

As Trevor slid into the chute, he thought to himself. It's *just a wild horse like I ride every day. I just need to stay on for eight seconds.* When the gate opened, the show was on. Trevor did manage to stay on for the eight seconds and appeared to be in control for the full ride. He was given a high score and he hoped it would be good enough to win. Lou and Jessie had both taken time to come and watch the event. Sure enough the score held, and Trevor had his second buckle.

Now bull riding was something Trevor had never done—when he got into the chute, he wondered if he had made a mistake. Steam was shooting out of the bull's nostrils and Trevor thought maybe he had bitten off more that he could handle. The gate was opened, and all hell broke loose. The only thing that kept Trevor on the bull for the full eight seconds was the fear of what would happen if he got bucked off. Again, to his amazement, he won the event and corresponding buckle. As he was the only rider to win three events, he was also given the all-around Cheyenne rodeo champion silver buckle.

Trevor had surpassed all of his expectations for his first rodeo. Someone had mentioned, "It's time to go to the dance and show off them buckles." Trevor decided to wear a baseball cap to the dance to try and keep a low profile, while checking the place out. Jessie was seated in a back corner, also hoping to keep a low profile and just enjoy the music and a few beers. It did not work for Trevor as Lou spotted him the minute he walked in. She wanted to dance, so Trevor agreed, and they hit the dance floor. Trevor had not held a girl since Susan, and it felt a little awkward, but also good.

Trevor was a fantastic dancer and Lou kept him to herself until about halfway through the dance, when some of her old boyfriends said that was enough and they wanted to dance with her. Trevor just about made it to a back corner when Jessie came up and asked if we would like to dance. She had obviously had a few beers, but she was steady enough to dance. Trevor really liked holding Jessie and they danced close, although he had to help her keep her balance on a couple of turns. He thought, how strange to be holding someone so close, other than Susan. Normally, Jessie would have just sat and listened to the music; however, the beers had overtaken her normal demeanor, and it was on to line dancing—then it was slow dancing and fast dancing as the evening progressed. Each slow dance, Trevor seemed to hold her tighter and tighter, and she did not seem to mind. At the end she was sneaking a kiss during each dance. Trevor was hoping it was not the beer talking, but that she was actually having a good time and enjoying being with him. He knew he was enjoying her, as she was built like a twenty-year-old and definitely felt good in his arms. It made him forget about Susan for a while.

He had never slept with a girl, except for his Shunga (Japanese art depicting pleasure of love) training.

Candy had arranged for two oriental girls who studied the art of Shunga, and then practiced it with Trevor in a Los Angeles hotel suite, as she felt he needed the experience. Trevor thought that maybe he would get lucky and be able to give his education a test. As the dance ended, Jessie said, "Why don't you come to my place for some coffee? I definitely need a cup to clear my head."

Jessie had a larger trailer on the fairground property, which was quite an improvement over Trevor's seventeen-foot sleeper trailer. She set about making the coffee as soon as they entered her place. Once she got the pot started, she came over to Trevor and gave him a big kiss. She thanked him for dancing so much, saying, "I really enjoyed it."

The next thing Trevor knew was that his shirt was being unbuttoned and slipped off his back. He reciprocated by doing the same for Jessie, and they soon found themselves in her bed. Trevor remembered his training and the first order of business was to satisfy Jessie, so the lesson he had learned was to go slow. It wasn't long before he had accomplished his objective, as it had apparently been awhile since she had been with a man and she was easily stimulated. After the first round Trevor was in control—several more times that night they made love until they both fell fast asleep.

"Oh my God," Trevor heard Jessie say. "I have overslept." Trevor grabbed her shoulder and said, "What's the rush?"

"You don't understand, cowboy. Now that the rodeo is over, we need to break down fences and store them in the sheds. People are waiting for me to tell them what to do. You shower and lock up, as I have to go right now," she said then scooted out the door.

Trevor took a shower, microwaved some of last night's coffee, and headed for work, as it was his job to help store the fencing. Most of the hands that had been working the rodeo grounds quickly put two and two together and had a few wise cracks to make, as they chuckled under their breath.

Trevor was not at full speed but was doing his best. Jason, one of the local helpers, asked if he had had a rough night and Trevor had ignored the question. "You are a lucky man," said Jason. "That does not happen very often—she is a great gal who works way too hard."

As the day progressed, it was business as usual and Jessie was back to her old self, with no mention of the night before. Although Trevor had thoroughly enjoyed it, he thought to himself, it must have just been a one-night stand that he would not soon forget. Jessie had mentioned earlier that a friend of her dad might have a need for a cowboy to break wild horses, on a ranch called the Silver Dollar. Jessie continued to ignore Trevor, so he decided it was time to move on. Jessie was headed to Laramie, Wyoming, to work at another rodeo and wanted to know if Trevor wanted to go, but he said he was headed for another mustang ranch to work with their horses. He asked for her phone number, and to his surprise she gave it to him. She put her arm around his neck and gave him a big kiss, saying, "Take care of yourself, cowboy."

Back at the Running Water Ranch, Susan had noticed an article about a cowboy named Trevor Tremaine winning the all-around cowboy title at the Cheyenne Rodeo. She noticed that he had also won a buckle with someone named Lou Hensley. She pointed it out to her mom and dad and Lilly said they knew the Hensley's from buying some cows from them years ago. "They own the Silver Dollar ranch close to Cheyenne. Trevor did pretty good at that rodeo; he probably headed for another one in some other part of the country." The subject was dropped, but Lilly could see that Susan's heart still belonged to Trevor.

Trevor arrived at the Silver Dollar ranch and asked to talk with Paul Hensley. He mentioned that Jessie Slocomb had said he might find work at Hensley's ranch. Trevor gave his references and Paul asked right away if John Fargo still owned the Running Water ranch. Trevor replied that yes, he did. Paul told Trevor that they had a trailer out in one of the fields adjacent to the ranch house and, if his references checked out, he could have the job of taking care of the barn and breaking a mustang whenever he had one rounded up.

"Oh, by the way, my wife's name is Sandra, and I have two daughters, Lou and Sunday." Trevor mentioned that he knew Lou from the Cheyenne Rodeo.

Paul did make a call to the Cheyenne Rodeo Association and to John Fargo, who gave Trevor a glowing recommendation. John and Lilly had decided not to tell Susan where Trevor was, as it would serve no purpose and only cause more heartache.

Trevor started shoveling manure after an early breakfast. He still had not been introduced to Sunday. Later that afternoon, two cowboys came riding in and one had been in an accident. Paul asked if Trevor would be willing to go into the back country to a small cabin, to capture and break wild mustangs. "You will probably be out there for a three-month period before you return to the ranch." Trevor said that would be great and he would love it.

So, Trevor rode out with Slim Granger, a cowboy about forty-five years old who looked to be hard as nails. Slim explained what they did and offered to let Trevor break as many of the horses as he wanted. He had ridden many in his day but, "it's a young man's game, you know." Trevor said, "No problem," as he had done similar work before.

As supplies were being delivered and horses were being sent back to the ranch at double the normal rate. Paul had been so surprised that he decided to go look for himself as to why so many horses were being broken at such a fast pace. Paul asked Sunday if she wanted to go for a ride up to the cabin and, as she had not ridden with her dad for some time, she said okay. When they arrived, Trevor was right in the middle of breaking one of the mustangs. Sunday was impressed with how good the cowboy was doing, as she recognized a good ride when she saw one. When the horse finally settled down and let Trevor ride him, he came over to where Paul and Sunday were standing.

"Good job, son," Paul said. "That was a good ride." Slim was standing close by and said, "He does that all day long. I have never seen such a good bronc rider in all my days."

"Yes," Paul said. "I have noted a large increase in the number of horses coming back to the ranch. We are having a slight problem finding buyers for the number of horses we are getting."

"I'll tell you what," Paul said. "Why don't you two come back to the ranch next week and we will call it a year. The Twin Star ranch down the road from us is having a big barbeque and dance to celebrate the end of the summer and all of my ranch hands are invited. However, you two had better clean up a little, as you look a little more than rough." They both said okay— they would like a break.

Sunday came over to Trevor and said, "There are only two conditions for you: Don't talk to me at the dance and don't ask me to dance. Got it?"

"Yes ma'am," Trevor said. Boy, I must really look bad, Trevor thought.

As Paul and Sunday rode away, Trevor found his cell phone and immediately called Candy. He explained the situation and told her he wanted to look like a million-dollar cowboy when he went to the dance. She said she would be there Saturday morning and to meet her in town.

Slim and Trevor arrived back at the ranch on Friday. Sunday and her best friend, Joyce Patterson, saw them come riding in with the last of the broken horses. Trevor went to his trailer to hopefully take a long shower. He had bathed in the river up by the cabin, but that was cold water, and he definitely wanted a hot shower.

Joyce mentioned to Sunday that "those two look pretty rough," and Sunday replied that she had told the younger one that he was not to talk or dance with her at the party, as she did not want to be embarrassed by the long haired, scruffy looking cowboy.

Trevor arrived in town and Candy was waiting right on schedule. Trevor would be nineteen in a few weeks and was filling out to be a handsome young man. She started laughing and said it appeared she did not have much to work with as he looked like hell. "First you are going to have a spa day and I promise to get you to the dance on time. We start with a haircut and shave, followed by a pedicure and manicure. We will then get you properly dressed; you will be ready to go."

Trevor kept giving her a slap on the butt and saying maybe he didn't want to go to the dance. Her reply was that the dance was the only possibility that he was going to get laid and to quit pestering her. Candy and Trevor had never been romantically involved; however, it was always fun to tease her. Candy was aware that Trevor would be nineteen in a few weeks and noticed he was filling out to be a handsome young man. He finally finished getting dressed and did not recognize himself in the mirror. Candy teased him with a comment that maybe he should stay with her and forget the dance—the fact that his hair had been dyed black and then cut extremely short to the hat line made it almost impossible to recognize Trevor from the cowboy that had ridden in on the day Sunday had given him his instructions. The top was still long but slicked back. A medium black mustache was left under his nose. "You cleaned up pretty good. Let's go, time to get this show on the road. I got you a little better truck to drive, so you're not recognized in that piece of crap you drive."

"Good idea and thanks for everything, Candy." He gave her a kiss on the cheek and said, "Wish me good luck."

As Trevor drove up the driveway of the Twin Star Ranch, no one seemed to notice. He got out of the truck and started walking up toward the house. Several of the young ladies and a few of the older ones immediately took notice of the good-looking stranger joining the party. The music was playing and a young lady named Paula, one of Sunday's best friends, got a head start by getting to Trevor first, asking if he would like to dance. Once she had her hands on him, she had no intention of letting him slip away with another girl.

Everyone could see that he was a good dancer and: "Oh my god, the way he fit into those jeans!"

Sunday could not understand why he would not ask her to dance, as she was sure she was the best looking and best dressed girl at the dance. Finally, she had to break in and get at least half a dance with this stranger. He held her tighter than she expected but his dancing was perfect. She ask him why he was holding her so tight, and his reply was, "Well ma'am, you are the prettiest girl at the dance, so why wouldn't I want to hold you tight?" With that response, she did not care how tight he held her.

As soon as the dance was over, Paula broke in to ask Trevor to be her dance partner for the next dance. Sunday gave her a nasty glare but conceded and walked away.

As soon as the dance was over, Trevor and Paula snuck off in his pickup to find a place to park. Paula had asked him earlier if he would like to get away from the dance for a while and have a few beers. Paula seemed to know where she wanted to go, so Trevor just drove. They wound up by a lake and watched the moon's reflection in the water. Candy had made sure the truck was equipped with a sleeping bag and several blankets in the back seat, and it was not long before Paula and Trevor were putting them to use in the back of the pickup.

Trevor got Paula home rather late, and her parents heard them drive in and heard Trevor leave. However, as Paula was almost twenty years old, no mention of the hour she arrived home was brought up in the morning. Trevor got home about four in the morning. He had really needed Paula last night, as he had been out in the back country for quite a lengthy time, and riding horses was just not the same kind of ride.

Sunday had heard Trevor drive in late but thought nothing about it. In the morning. Sunday was still upset that the young cowboy at the dance had not asked her to dance. She wanted to ask Trevor if he was at the dance and if he had noticed her. She went to his trailer and knocked lightly on the door. She wanted to make sure he was by himself, as she did not recognize the pickup by the trailer. Trevor covered his head with a pillow and said, "Come in," as the door was unlocked.

"Trevor, did you notice me at the dance last night?"

"Yes," was Trevor's reply.

"Do you think I was dressed nice and looked pretty?"

"Yes ma'am, you were the prettiest girl at the dance."

Sunday felt grateful and happy with the reply, even though it came from Trevor. "Did you notice the good-looking cowboy at the dance, dancing mostly with Paula?"

"Yes, I did" Trevor replied.

"I cannot figure out why he did not ask me to dance and why he would not talk with me."

"I guess you would have to ask him yourself to find out," was Trevor's reply.

"Well, thank you," Sunday said, as she left and walked back toward the ranch house.

As she passed through the kitchen, she stopped dead in her tracks. "I am going to kill him. You have got to be shitting me."

Sandra said, "Language, Sunday." Sunday remembered the comment of "Well ma'am, you are the prettiest girl at the dance." She had heard those words at the dance the night before. She spun around and stomped out the door, headed for Trevor's trailer. This time she stomped right up to the door and just about busted the door getting it open. Trevor had again put the pillow over his head and pretended to be asleep. Sunday began tugging at the pillow and finally mounted Trevor's back trying to pull the pillow off, so she could see his face. In the tussle, she wound up on her side, facing Trevor. He let the pillow slip and she saw who it was. He proceeded to give her a big kiss against her wishes. "What was that all about?" she said. Trevor's reply was, "I just wanted to kiss the most beautiful girl who was at the dance last night."

Sunday was so flustered, she pushed herself away and headed for the ranch house. She stormed into the living room where her mom and dad were sitting and demanded that Trevor be fired immediately. Her mom wanted to know what happened and she said, "He kissed me!"

About that time, Trevor wandered into the kitchen to grab an apple and Paul asked him to come into the living room. He asked if Trevor had kissed his daughter. Trevor replied, "Yes."

"Why did you do that?"

"Well sir, this beautiful young lady stomped up to my trailer while I was sleeping in my bed and almost busted my door down. She then mounted me as though I was a horse and proceeded to pull at my pillow. During the tussle, she wound up lying at my side, and the pillow came off. I figured with all that effort, she was looking for something, so I gave her a kiss. Besides, I wanted to kiss the most beautiful girl that was at the dance last night. I don't believe I did anything wrong."

"Sunday, why were you doing all of this?" her dad asked.

"He wouldn't dance or talk with me at last night's dance, and I could not figure out why." Trevor reminded her that when she invited him to the dance, she told him not to talk or dance with her. She sort of shrugged her shoulders and said, "Do you really think I was the most beautiful girl at the dance?" Trevor took a big bite out of his apple and said, "Maybe." As he went out the door, Sunday was right behind him saying, "Come on Trevor, tell me the truth."

"Well," Paul said, "I guess we don't have to worry about firing him right now—seems the problem has been solved."

Sandra said, "That boy is going to be trouble. Did you see the glint in his eyes as he left the house? Those two have not had their last battle, as they seem to be developing a little chemistry."

Later that day, Paula Jackson, one of Sunday's best friends, called to tell her about her night with Trevor, not knowing Sunday had taken a sudden interest in Trevor. It took about one minute for Sunday to again want Trevor fired. "You went where?" Sunday almost shouted into the phone. "You did what?" Sunday didn't know what to say—her best friend spent the night in the back of Trevor's pickup looking at the stars. She was flabbergasted.

"Yes, it surprised me too, and I may be grounded, as I did not get in until well after three a.m., but it was worth it," said Paula. Sunday made up an excuse to cut the phone call short and proceeded to smolder. "Yeah, I'll bet they were looking at the stars."

"Who was that, dear?" Sunday's mom asked.

"I want him fired first thing in the morning," was the only thing Sunday could say. "Do you know he spent the night out with Paula in the back of his pickup enjoying the moon, stars, and each other?! Paula just told me all about it."

"Why is that any concern of yours, Sunday? You are not going out with Trevor, you know."

Sunday left the house and headed straight for Trevor's trailer to confront him. "That kiss you gave me this morning; did it mean anything?"

"I told you I wanted to kiss the most beautiful girl at the dance," was Trevor's reply.

"Well, it seems like you had time to take Paula out parking," she said.

"Yes, we went out for a while, but why are you asking?"

"Did you have a good time?" Sunday asked.

"We had a great time. I always have a good time when I am out with a girl under the stars."

Sunday didn't know what to say. She just turned and walked back to the house. As she stormed through the kitchen, her dad hollered at her: "What is the verdict—is he hired or fired?" After that, all he heard was the slamming of her bedroom door.

The next day, Sunday came to the barn to ask Trevor if he would like to go for a trail ride with her in the afternoon, and he replied that he would have to take a rain check as he already had plans. "Oh, come on," Sunday said. "It's a beautiful day for a trail ride."

"I am already going with Paula to some hot springs that are on her dad's ranch, and she said it would take most of the afternoon." Trevor noticed that Sunday was not pleased with the answer she got. She had heard stories about those hot springs and did not like the thought of Trevor and Paula being there.

Sunday had to figure out a way for Trevor to pay more attention to her and forget about Paula. Fortunately, college was about to begin, and Trevor would have to wait, as Sunday would have to focus on school. It was only about six weeks into the school term that Trevor got a letter from Sunday, telling him she had met a boy she liked and would be bringing him home to meet her parents. This came as no surprise to Trevor, as these things happen when daughters go off to school. It's always party time at school and new friendships are developed.

The good news buzzing around the ranch was that Lou was coming home for a few days. Trevor was looking forward to her visit. She was bringing a friend that she had met in the rodeo and whom Trevor knew, Jessie Slocomb. Trevor was looking forward to Jessie's visit even though they had parted under strange circumstances.

When Lou arrived, she went straight into the house to say hello to her parents. She had been gone from the ranch for quite some time and tears were flowing freely. Paul said, "Boy, that young man Jessie sent us was really a good find. He does the work of two people and never complains." Lou had to think for a moment and said, "You mean Trevor?"

"Yes, of course," Paul said.

"Where is he?" Lou asked.

"Well, I assume he is out in the barn."

"I am going to say hello," Lou said, as she went out the front door.

Upon entering the barn, she spotted Trevor and walked over and gave him a big hug. "Hello cowboy, how you been doing?" Trevor told her about most of the summer events and said coming to the Silver Dollar Ranch was the best thing that could have happened to him. "After spending the summer here at the ranch, I really learned to ride wild horses—going to a rodeo and bronc riding are much easier."

After a while, Lou returned to the house and Sandra asked her how she'd met Trevor and how long she had known him. "We met at a rodeo, and I needed a partner in the calf roping and he agreed to help and we won. That's about all I know about him."

Jessie arrived later that day and all the family went out to greet her. Trevor was not aware that Jessie had practically grown up on the Hensley's ranch as a child, and Jessie always called Sandra "Mom." When Jessie saw Trevor coming out of the barn, she was a bit surprised, but remembered suggesting he look for work at the Silver Dollar. She walked over and gave him a big hug. "I was not expecting to see you here," she said. "But it is nice to see you again."

All the girls went into the ranch kitchen, while Trevor went about his chores. "Okay," Sandra said, "spill the beans."

"Well, what do you mean, Mom?" was Jessie's reply.

"You don't go round giving hugs to strangers, so what's the story?" Jessie told most of the story, leaving out the one-night stand; however, she did say, "That cowboy is trouble."

"So, you got hooked and ran away like you always do," said Sandra.

"Something like that," was Jessie's reply.

As a few days passed, Paul asked Sandra what was going on between Jessie and Trevor, as they always seemed to be horsing around on the grounds outside or in the field, often trying to rope one another or splashing water on each other as they were taking care of the horses. "Just horse play," was Sandra's response.

"Seems to be more than that to me," was Paul's comment.

"Just mind your own business," was Sandra's reply.

It was only a week before Christmas and Sunday was about to arrive with her new boyfriend. Trevor and Jessie had gotten very close during Jessie's stay. She had actually postponed leaving a couple times for various reasons. Sandra knew Jessie was falling for Trevor, and the same seemed true for Trevor. The age difference did not seem to matter—they were like two high school teenagers falling in love.

Sunday and her new friend, Matt Young, arrived two days before Christmas and Sunday, Lou, Sandra, and Jessie were busy in the kitchen. Jessie was especially happy, as she and Trevor had slipped a little the night before and spent the night in Trevor's trailer. The love making was just as she had remembered, and she had no regrets the next morning. Sandra knew something had happened as Jessie snuck in the back door of the house and went straight to her room for a good shower.

Jessie knew that she had already missed breakfast, so she would just make up an excuse and find herself a bowl of cereal. As she entered the kitchen, Sandra asked if she had slept well last night. "I was fine, Mom," with a slight grin across her face.

"I'll bet you were," Sandra replied. "You had better make Trevor a bowl also, as he is probably hungry, too."

Later that day, Sunday was talking to Jessie regarding the frosting on the cookies. "Earth calling Jessie; earth calling Jessie. Where were you? You didn't hear a word I said."

"Sorry," Jessie replied. "I was just thinking about my life and what I wanted to do with it. I sort of spaced out."

Sandra said, "Yes, Jessie has a lot thinking to do." Her tone was a little rough, as she was not liking the Jessie and Trevor thing, because of the age difference. She felt it was just a fling that would soon disappear when life got in the way.

Although Sunday was with Matt Young, she could not help noticing Trevor, and the old attraction began to slip back into her thoughts. She told herself she could not let that happen, but here she was again looking at the million-dollar cowboy. Sandra noticed the attention Sunday was paying to Trevor, so she took her aside and said she needed to stay on her side of the fence, as Jessie and Trevor were working some things out. Sunday's teeth about fell out of her mouth. "You mean Trevor and Jessie have a thing for one another?" Sunday said.

"You could probably call it more than a thing, but I believe it will work itself out. In the meantime, stay away from Trevor."

It was Christmas Eve and Trevor had been invited to the main house for dinner and after dinner festivities. Everyone ate way more than they should have, and Sandra announced it was time for some Christmas carols. Paul got out his guitar and started strumming "Oh Holy Night." Trevor got up from the couch and walked over to the old piano sitting in the corner. He found an old Christmas carol book and soon joined in.

The voices grew louder, and the music could probably be heard in the next county. When all was done, Jessie said, "I did not know you could play the piano." Trevor replied, "I just picked up a little here and there. I am glad you liked it."

Sandra said, "I just wish you knew 'Chopin-Etude Op 10 No. 3'—it's my favorite of all piano pieces." Trevor sat back down at the piano and began to play with no music in front of him. Everyone was astonished and Sandra was delighted. He kept thinking he should stop, but everyone was glued to their seats—especially Sandra.

Finally, Trevor stopped and said Merry Christmas to Sandra. She did not know what to say. She went to give Trevor a big hug as tears rolled down her face, causing everyone in the room to become teary eyed. "I don't know who you are, Trevor Tremaine, but with a talent like that you definitely should not be working as a ranch hand."

"Where did you learn to play like that?" Jessie asked. Trevor just said, "Oh you pick up and little here and there." Trevor decided it was getting late and he should be getting back to his trailer, so Jessie escorted him out onto the porch. Sunday was peeking out the window and Jessie said she would be at his trailer as soon as she could sneak out. She gave Trevor an "I want to know you better kiss," and Trevor left.

"Wow," Sunday said as Jessie came back into the house. "That was one hell of a kiss. It almost made me have to go change my pants."

"Mind your own business, Sunday," Jessie said.

"No way, you have to give me all the details," Sunday said.

Jessie said, "I like him and we are just friends." Then she added: "with benefits," as a small grin came across her face. Sunday flipped out. "You got to be kidding me. Come on—tell me all the details." Jessie said she did not have time as there was someplace she had to be.

Jessie went to her room, opened the window, and made her exit. It wasn't long before Sunday came to check on Jessie in her room and, sure enough, she was gone. Sunday went to the kitchen to find her mom to see if she knew where Jessie was. Sandra said, "Oh, she's probably in Trevor's trailer."

"And you're okay with that?" Sunday said.

"Mind your own business, Sunday. You should get ready for Christmas morning. And Sunday, you are not to lock Jessie's window and spoil Christmas—just let it go."

Christmas morning, Jessie snuck back into her room and found Sunday was fast asleep in Jessie's bed. Jessie woke her and said she needed to leave right now as she had to get into her Christmas pajamas and go to the living room to open packages with the family. Trevor had not been invited, as everyone was sure that Paul was not aware of Jessie and Trevor's activities. When everyone was there and ready to open the presents, Paul said "Wait a minute. Where is Trevor? Shouldn't he be here, or wouldn't he fit through Jessie's bedroom window?" Jessie immediately jumped up and said, "Thank you so much—I will go get him."

Trevor was already dressed and shoveling manure in the barn. "Come on Trevor, the family wants you to come to the gift package opening."

She was so happy she gave him a kiss and headed for the house. "Wait Jessie, come and help me with my packages, as I have too many to carry by myself." They soon arrived at the house and the gift exchange began. Trevor had gotten Jessie a beautiful set of diamond earrings that obviously cost way too much for a normal gift. She ask why he had gotten such an expensive gift and his reply was that Paul paid him a lot of money and she was worth it. Sunday couldn't wait to open her gift from Trevor, but it was only a fancy pair of riding gloves.

When the gift exchange was over, the girls all headed for the kitchen to prepare the morning brunch. Sunday came over by Jessie and said, "You know Jessie, this little fling you are having can't go anywhere as there is too large an age difference. You should break it off and both move on before one of you gets seriously hurt."

"The only thing that is hurting me now is you, Sunday. How can you say such a hurtful thing to me? I have done nothing to cause you to hurt me so." Jessie said.

"I am not trying to hurt you, Jessie. I am just being practical. Where do you see this going, anyway?" Sunday asked. He's almost twenty and you're almost twenty-seven.

The rest of the morning was spent enjoying Christmas, except Trevor noticed the girls seemed to be avoiding one another. Jessie did spend the night with Trevor, but she had been thinking about what

Sunday had said. Jessie made a few phone calls and then, around the dinner table, she announced she had taken a job at a rodeo in Billings, Montana. She said it was time to get back to work and this job opportunity had come up, so she took it. "I am going to the barn to tell Trevor and I will be leaving in the morning." Sunday felt sorry for Jessie and hoped the things she had said were not the cause of Jessie's decision to leave.

Jessie entered the barn and Trevor gave her a big hug and asked, "What's up?" She told him she would be leaving in the morning for a job she had taken in Montana. Trevor was not expecting her to be leaving and he was in shock. "Why?" Trevor asked. "I thought we had a good thing going here and that you were happy with me."

"I am Trevor, but it's time to move on." She tried to give him back the expensive earrings, but he said, "No way. They were a gift to a dear friend." Trevor knew in the back of his mind that she was right, but it still hurt and did not relieve the pain he was feeling. "Thank you for everything, Trevor. I do love you so much." She turned and walked away, leaving Trevor with tears in his eyes—but nothing compared to those streaming down Jessie's face.

Chapter 8

*T*revor thanked Paul and Sandra for having him at the ranch, but the pain of Jessie's leaving put Trevor on the road again. He again had a discussion with himself, trying to decide what he wanted to do with his life—he had the world to choose from. He had accomplished all of his objectives, with the exception of finding true love. Somehow this goal had eluded him, which may have been because of his young age. He decided to continue as a ranch hand because he had met such interesting people and because he liked the work he was doing. He found himself at the Pendleton Round Up, a rodeo in Pendleton, Oregon. He was still hurting from Jessie's leaving for Montana and again looking for short term work to keep him busy and to participate in the Pendleton rodeo. He was not very well known in Oregon, so his entry into the bronc and bull riding events did not cause any attention. He again was able to find work in the stock area of the rodeo and a place to sleep in an old trailer—seems that was his new life pattern.

He checked out the horse, Devil's Churn, and bull, Sunday Delight, trying to learn as much as possible by talking to other riders that would be participating at the event. He was only able to get some very sketchy information, but it was better than nothing at all. Neither animal had been ridden for the full eight seconds, which spoke volumes as to what he should expect.

When Trevor's name was spotted by the announcer, he immediately knew who Trevor Tremaine was. He said "Oh my gosh, folks—have we got a special treat for you tonight. Trevor Tremaine is one of the better bronc and bull riders in North America. He must have snuck in on us."

About that time, Trevor was slipping into the chute to mount Devil's Churn. When the gate opened, Trevor thought maybe he had picked a horse that would finally get the best of him; however, he did manage to go the eight seconds and eventually the buckle was his.

The same was true for Sunday Delight—although Trevor felt it was a close call on the eight seconds. The judges said he made it, but Trevor did wind up on the ground before the pickup rider could get him off the bull. He found himself scrambling for the fence with one angry bull trying to rip a hole in the back of his pants. Trevor thought, "I hope the buckle was worth it." Trevor knew it was not about the buckle, but a way to temporarily forget about Jessie. At least Jessie had left his thoughts for a moment, as he was scrambling for his life.

The dance that followed was the best part of the day. Trevor loved to dance and as he walked into the dance hall, several young ladies came his way—it appeared his dance card would be full for the night. While dancing, Trevor noticed this one girl standing against the wall, who did not seem to be dancing at all. She was dressed very plainly, and her hair was just in a simple ponytail. She was very thin and did not appear to be wearing much makeup. Trevor would guess her age to be in her early twenties. He thought he should go and ask her to dance the next dance.

As he approached her, he noted that she was very nervous. He asked if she would like to dance and she nodded yes. Before they started, she showed him a note that said she stuttered, so she would not be trying to talk. Trevor said, "Fine, let's get to it." He said he might ask simple questions that she could nod her head yes or no to so they could communicate.

She was an above average dancer and had apparently had lessons. As they floated among the other dancers, she eventually began to relax a little and started to enjoy the dance. They danced several dances and eventually Trevor said, "Let's take a break."

She pulled out a small pad from a pocket in her dress and wrote her name was Becky Clarino. She lived on a pig farm just outside town, called the Bacon BBQ. A waltz started to play, so Trevor ask if she could waltz. She nodded her head, and they took to the dance floor. Not many people waltzed, so they had the dance floor to themselves.

Her father Tim was also there; when he finally noticed her dancing with the young cowboy, a tear came to his eyes. Although he was overprotective of her, he knew his late wife would be so proud of the way she was dancing and moving about the floor and of the young lady she had become. He really had a hard time raising a daughter by himself—he tried the best he could, but he really did not have much of a social life as an overweight pig farmer, and the fact that his daughter stuttered did not help her either. They'd pretty much stayed on the farm and kept to themselves for most of their lives. After the dance, Trevor said goodbye to Becky and Tim Clarino. Trevor did ask if it would be all right if he came out to the farm to ask her out on a date, and both said that would be fine.

A couple of days later, Trevor located the pig farm and went to see if Becky would go on a date with him. Becky and her dad came out to greet him, both dressed in overalls and baseball hats. Becky was a little embarrassed at her appearance, but Trevor said: "Don't worry; I look about the same when I am cleaning out the barn in the morning." He wanted to take her for dinner and an opera in town and she nodded yes; however, she wrote on the pad that she did not have fancy clothes to wear any place grand. Trevor said, "I have just what you need, and her name is Candy Wade. She will be here to pick you up early Saturday morning and she will take care of all your needs."

When Becky went to the bathroom, Trevor told Tom that Becky would probably be gone all day, but he would have her home about midnight. Mr. Clarino said, "She is all I have, so please take good care of her."

Trevor said, "Not to worry, we are going out to have a good time and I will bring her back safe and sound. One thing I would like to say, Mr. Clarino, is that I thought horse manure smelled bad, but you definitely have me beat in the smell department."

Mr. Clarino laughed and said, "That is the smell of money, son!"

Trevor told Becky what would be happening with Candy and then left to return to the Pendleton fair grounds. After a spa day in Pendleton on Saturday, Candy drove Becky to the Pendleton airport. Becky was dressed in an elegant dress and cape suitable for dining and the opera. Becky wrote a note to Candy saying she had never felt so beautiful.

Trevor met Becky and Candy in Portland, Oregon. Becky had no idea that she was being flown to Portland for her date when Trevor had said an opera in town.

Trevor could not believe how beautiful Becky looked and her dress was so stunning. Trevor told her how beautiful she looked, and she paused for a moment and said with a stutter: "Thank you." She did not even resemble the pig farmer's daughter. Candy would get a bonus for the wonderful job she had done.

The opera playing was *The Barber of Seville*, and after dinner in the fanciest restaurant Becky had ever seen in her life, it was time to move on to the Arlene Schnitzer Concert Hall. Trevor was not really an opera fan, but watching Becky all night brought him great joy. He knew she could not understand a word being sung, but he knew she was feeling the passion and love being played out on the stage. Tears were flowing down her cheeks as the performance went along. Trevor realized she was so absorbed by the performance; she did not even know he was there.

As they were leaving and she had dried her eyes, they ran into Robert Grey, who was an old friend of Becky's. They talked for a few moments, mostly in sign language, as he was also speech impaired—actually, Robert was telling Becky how beautiful she looked, as he had never seen her so dressed up in such a beautiful gown. They had a long history in school and had developed feelings for one another early in life.

After getting flown home around midnight, Trevor went to her side of the truck to let her out. She stopped at the door and composed herself and said—all without stuttering: "Thank you very much. I had a wonderful evening." She had practiced all day and hoped it would come out correct. Trevor said, "Perfect," and gave her a good night kiss.

Trevor was a bit surprised, as there did not seem to be much emotion in the kiss. She then turned and went into the house. It almost made Trevor feel as though he had done something wrong. He pondered that kiss all the way home and finally just let it go.

The next morning, Trevor got a call from Mr. Clarino who said he was calling for Becky. "She wanted you to know that she had one of the best times of her life yesterday, but her heart belongs to Robert Grey, who I believe you met last night. They don't see each other very often, as they both have communication problems, but she says you have taught her that a speech impediment is not a real problem that should make her hide on the farm. I am sorry, Trevor, but that is what she wanted me to call and tell you. Thank you for taking care of my little girl."

Trevor was glad Mr. Clarino had told him this, as it explained the kiss; however, Trevor could not let this go. He asked around and soon located Robert Grey— he was the son of a very prominent family in the small town of Hood River, Oregon.

Trevor went to the door of what was considered a very upscale home. A maid answered the door and Trevor asked to speak with Robert Grey. As Trevor was carrying a tablet and pencil, the maid was aware that

Trevor knew about Robert's speech problem. Trevor was invited into the parlor and Robert soon arrived with a tablet and pencil in hand. Trevor reminded him that they had met at the opera a couple days before. Since he was dressed in ranch clothes versus a tux, Trevor was not sure that Robert would remember. Trevor said he was there to ask Robert a very personal question and that he did not have to answer. Trevor wanted to know if Robert had any personal feelings for Becky Clarino.

"Why do you ask?" Robert wrote. "First you have to answer my question and then I will answer yours," was Trevor's reply. Robert wrote that he had known Becky since the fourth grade, and they had become close friends but did not get to see one another very often since he moved from the Pendleton area. "It's hard for us to communicate, other than by computer. I do like her very much and thought she was exceptionally beautiful at the opera. What is she to you?" Robert asked.

"We are just friends and I wanted to give her the opportunity to go to an opera, so we had a dinner date and that was all. I am not a boyfriend, just a friend," Trevor replied.

Robert said, "I should make a greater effort to get reacquainted, as we were true friends."

"I know she is also fond of you, Robert, and the purpose of my visit was to see if you also had an interest in her. I think you two should get to know each other again. If you do care, you should drive out to her farm and talk with her. You might find you have more in common than the fact that communication is a little more difficult for you than for other people. I will be leaving now for Montana, but I just could not go without trying to get you two together." As Trevor drove away, he knew that everything was going to get better for Becky and Robert.

Chapter 9

*T*revor pulled into the town of Bozeman, Montana. He was hoping to complete his certification at Montana State University that would allow him to volunteer in a hospital nursery to care for newborn babies. He was not looking for a job, just the opportunity to learn what it took to take care of a young child. He had always wanted to do this; however, he did not realize it took so much education to become certified.

He had been taking online education courses for a couple of years, as time allowed, but now he needed the practical experience to finish what he had started. Besides, he was getting discouraged at being a ranch hand and at his failure to connect with girls in such a way as to feel he had a true girlfriend. Relationships did not appear to be his forte and a little change might do him some good.

He stopped at the Handgun Bar and Grill for a burger and noticed a fine-looking young lady taking orders. Old habits made him look, but other than that, he told himself to leave it alone. He had grabbed a newspaper as he had come in and was looking in the wanted ads for some type of work to keep him occupied on a part time basis—nothing was listed for the type of work he wanted.

Trevor noticed that Peggy was the name on the waitress tag as she took his order. She asked what he was doing in this part of the country. Trevor said he was looking for part time work but did not see much listed. "What type of work do you do?" she asked.

"I can do anything, but I prefer being outdoors doing labor type of work."

She looked him over and said, "Maybe I can help you out a little." She said she would place his order and make a couple phone calls to see if anyone knew of part time work. It wasn't long before she returned with his order and a note that said, "Broken Arrow Ranch, Nate Fuller." She said to go to this ranch and they might be able to help him out. He said, "Thank you," and introduced himself as Trevor Tremaine. She paid him no further notice and went about her business. Trevor thought, she probably thinks I am trying to hit on her, so he let it go when she showed no interest.

Although Trevor had wanted to try some different type of work, the life of the ranch hand would not let go of him. He located the ranch only five miles out of town and thought to himself, *this would be great if he could get a job this close to town and the university.*

Nate Fuller had been holding a horse in the corral waiting for Trevor Tremaine to arrive for his interview. When Trevor arrived, they made a little small talk and then Nate said he was looking for someone to break a few horses. It would be about half a day's work with the rest of the day off. Trevor said great, as he was trying to attend some classes at Montana State and would appreciate the flexibility of schedule.

"Well, let's just go over here and complete your interview. This little guy's name is Shooting Star. We have not had anyone able to stay on him long enough to even think about breaking him down. Want to give it a go?"

"Let's do It," Trevor said. It took about five seconds and Trevor found himself in the unusual position of landing on his face with a mouth full of dirt.

Trevor got up and said, "Put him back in the chute." Trevor's pride was hurt, as he had not been thrown off a horse in some time.

"All right, it's your body," said Nate. The second time around went much smoother, and it took about a minute or two for Shooting Star to give up. He was now trotting around the corral with Trevor in control. "Well, I guess you are hired," Nate said.

Trevor was shown to a small bunkhouse adjacent to the barn, where he unloaded his truck. Nate said, "We don't always have horses to ride, so when that happens, just turn the horses out and muck out the barn, feed, and water them as needed, and the rest of the day is yours. Pay is minimal and food is provided in the main house. There are two other ranch hands that work here and I will introduce you to them at dinner."

Peggy didn't know why, but she took the time to call her brother, Nate, to see how the cowboy she sent him did in his interview. "I think you sent me a real winner," was Nate's reply. "And he is now working at the Broken Arrow Ranch."

Trevor met Billy Jackson and Ralph Numen at dinner. They were both old rodeo cowboys that were retired and just did routine ranch work on a part time basis. Ralph asked, "You're not the Trevor Tremaine of rodeo fame, are you?"

Trevor said, "Guilty as charged; however, I wouldn't say I was famous."

Nate said, "Wait, you're a known rodeo cowboy?"

Ralph interrupted and said, "He is one of the top rodeo cowboys in today's events. He probably has enough buckles to fill a suitcase."

Nate said he did not know, as he did not really follow rodeo. Trevor said, "Please, can we keep this among us? I don't want to be treated as special by anyone, and that is usually what happens when word spreads as to who I am. I don't want all the attention that comes with the name."

Trevor had been working well at the ranch and had made arrangements at Montana State University to come in on Thursday evenings to start his supervised practical training. The weekend arrived, and to Trevor's surprise, Peggy showed up at the ranch and went straight to the ranch house. Nate later pointed out that Peggy was his sister. He said he also had another sister, Faith. They would probably both be at dinner, as Faith often came home on the weekends from school. "It is odd for Peggy to be here, as ranching is not really her thing; however, Faith is all about ranching and is going for a veterinary degree. She has a wild side and likes to party a lot—drives my dad nuts."

"Where are your parents?" Trevor asked, as he had not seen them around the ranch.

"Oh, they are on vacation moving about the states in a motor home. They should be back next week."

At dinner that night, Trevor was introduced to both girls. He had to admit one thing and that was that both the girls were from a fine gene pool. Peggy was a little calmer, but she did like to talk about her life plan and how it was going to take her away from the ranch. Faith was just the opposite, talking about improvements that could be made around the ranch.

When Trevor got up to take his dishes to the sink, he could hear both of the girls talking about how his ass fit in those jeans he was wearing. As far as Trevor was concerned, they were just standard jeans and no big deal. He figured they were just having girl talk and he would ignore them. As he left the room to go back to the bunk house, he looked over his shoulder with a smile and told the girls to put their eyes back in their heads.

Trevor was up early with Nate, as they were going to break a horse named Diamond Dollar. He had been giving Billy and Ralph a tough time, so now it was Trevor's turn. Faith filled her coffee cup and then proceeded to the corral to watch. Diamond Dollar was truly a rough one, but Trevor managed to stay on until the horse eventually trotted around the arena, indicating he had given up.

Faith was totally impressed with the ride, as she knew when a cowboy had done a good job. She was definitely going to have to get to know this cowboy better—he was not only good looking but could really ride a horse.

Peggy came to the barn later when Trevor was mucking out a stall and asked him to saddle up a horse so she could go for a trail ride up into the mountains. Trevor said, "Sorry ma'am—it's not in my job description. Besides, I am sure you know how to put tack on a horse."

Peggy went fuming back to the ranch house, passing Nate on the way. "What's the matter, sis?" he asked.

"I asked that arrogant ranch hand I sent you to saddle a horse for me and he refused. Who in the hell does he think he is? He said it's not in his job description."

"I'll go saddle you a horse," Nate said.

She replied, "Don't bother; I am not in the mood now." Peggy stopped on the front porch long enough to hear Faith ask Trevor to saddle a couple horses so they could go on a trail ride together. He replied no problem and headed for the barn to get the horses. Peggy went into the house, slamming the door to make herself feel better.

It wasn't long before Harold and Joyce Fuller arrived back home at the ranch. Trevor was introduced during dinner. Harold wanted to know if he was the rodeo cowboy, and he said, "Yes." Peggy and Faith had not been told this information, so Nate said everyone was to keep this information under their hat.

Peggy had gone into the kitchen to talk with her mom about Trevor's refusal to saddle a horse for her. She was still pissed about the whole affair.

"Well, don't you know how to saddle your own horse?" Joyce asked. "How did he get hired at the ranch?" Joyce wanted to know.

"I asked Nate to give him an interview and I guess he got hired."

"Well dear, I will talk with Nate about it, and we'll get it all straightened out."

Going to MSU for practical training was a blast. The RNs would bring one of the little babies into each class, but never more than five babies at a time. Students would get to hold them, change them, feed them, and most importantly learn how to wrap them in the blankets.

Trevor was the only male in the class and often was the subject of jokes and small talk among the female nurses and students. One nurse, Alice Moore, seemed to pay a little more attention to Trevor than the other nurses. She was a petite blonde who often wore her hair in a bobbing little ponytail—she always seemed to be so full of energy. She would often tell Trevor he was not wrapping the baby correctly and would take the time to show him the correct way, while bumping into him an inordinate number of times. Trevor enjoyed the extra attention and the smiles that came with it. He kept telling himself she was hitting on him, but he was also trying to keep everything professional.

At twenty-two years of age, Trevor had grown into a totally handsome young man and often had women checking his hand to see if a ring was present. One night after class, Trevor asked Alice if she would like to go for coffee after her shift and she said, "Sure." Trevor waited around until her shift was over and they then went to an all-night dinner. They talked much longer than they should have, trying to get to know one another.

Trevor arrived home at the ranch at about four a.m.. Peggy had heard him come in and wondered where he had been all night. Trevor was late getting up the next morning, but Nate said it was no problem—he had just done other chores while waiting for Trevor to arrive.

Peggy was out by the stables and asked Trevor if he was a little groggy after getting in so late. Trevor said he had a lot of schoolwork to do and lost track of time. Peggy was thinking, "I'll bet you did." She realized Trevor was quite attractive and probably had several girlfriends. Why did she care? She had a life plan, and it did not include falling for a ranch hand.

Faith came out and asked if Trevor wanted to go for a trail ride, but he said he had work to do with Nate and to check later. "Good," thought Peggy. "I am not the only one he says no to!" However, later in the day Trevor came out of the barn with two saddled horses and asked Faith if she still wanted to go for that ride. Faith said no, she had plans, even though she did not. She was just getting even for being turned down earlier in the day.

Trevor turned to Peggy and asked if she would like to go. Faith began to sputter a little, thinking maybe she should have gone. Peggy said, "Sounds like fun—let's go."

They rode up to Trout Lake and decided to sit and watch the lake for a while. The lake lay dead flat, and the afternoon winds had not yet caused the ripples and waves that would soon appear on the water surfaces. The birds sang as they went about their daily business of securing food. The clouds that floated calmly in the early afternoon skies indicated that the temperatures would be pleasant for all to enjoy. The reflection of the mountains and trees in the lake water added to the calming effect that was just what Peggy needed to relax and enjoy her day. Looking across the lake you could see the green pathways cut among the trees, just waiting for the winter snow to cover the green foliage with white snow, inviting the winter skiers for the winter season.

Peggy could not believe that she was actually enjoying herself with Trevor. They both had gone from sitting to laying on the blanket and looking up at the white clouds, trying to imagine different figures in the shapes floating by. Peggy finally said, "We had better get started back so we get back before it gets dark." Trevor, too, had enjoyed the afternoon and hoped they could do it again sometime.

Faith had been waiting for Peggy's return, her mind racing with different thoughts and emotions as to what Peggy and Trevor could have been doing. It was about time for dinner, so Trevor was going to take care of the horses and Peggy was going to help with dinner. Suddenly, this little girl came running from the house, yelling: "Mommy, Mommy!" She then threw her arms around Peggy's neck. Peggy gave her four-and-a-half year old daughter a big hug and asked if she was helping her grandma with dinner. "Yes, I am, but she wants you to come and help, too."

Peggy's ex-husband had dropped Annie off at the ranch as scheduled. She always liked to come to her grandma's house so she could play with all the animals. It wasn't long before Annie had found her way to the barn and Trevor. She wanted to know if she could ride a pony and Trevor asked if it was okay with her mom. "Yes, it's okay," said Annie.

"Well, you sure talk well for such a little girl," Trevor said. "Which horse do you like to ride?" and she pointed to Snowbird.

"That's a pretty big horse for such a little cowgirl," Trevor said.

"Well, Mommy leads the horse around and I just hold on," Annie said.

"Well, let's put a saddle on him and see how you do."

"We don't use a saddle," Annie said.

"Well, let's put one on anyway," said Trevor. They walked into the back pen, with Annie talking all the way. Trevor was thinking—this must be the mouth that never stops. "You sure talk a lot for such a little girl. Don't you ever take a break?"

"I have a lot to say," was Annie's reply.

Trevor lifted her up onto Snowbird's back and began leading her around the corral. Trevor could tell she was not particularly good at holding on and suspected she had lied about pony rides. Peggy came out of the house looking for Annie and asked her dad if he had seen her. He said, "I saw her go into the barn. Let's go check it out." As Peggy and Harold got toward the back of the barn, they could hear Annie talking and then saw Annie and Trevor in the corral. Peggy stepped forward getting ready to run when Peggy's dad grabbed her arm. "I am going to kill him," came out of Peggy's mouth.

"Hold on," her dad said. "Let's watch for a minute."

Annie was laughing so loud that Trevor did not hear Peggy and her dad in the barn. "Let's go faster, Trevor! Let's go faster!"

"We are going fast enough; you have to learn to hold on better before we can go faster." Trevor said. "Squeeze Snowbird's sides a little tighter with your legs and it will help you to sit up straight and keep your balance. Now watch when I pull the rein to the left— she goes this way, and when I pull the rein to the right, she goes this way. When you pull back on the reins, she stops. That's the first and most important thing to learn. Whenever you are in trouble and maybe going a little too fast, you pull back on the reins and the horse will slow down or stop. You need to learn to talk to the horse with your body and not your mouth, then she will know what you want her to do. I think that's enough for today so maybe we should take Snowbird back into the barn and take care of her."

"Just a little bit more," she begged and when Trevor said "All right," she started laughing her head off again as she was having so much fun.

"All right, time to go," said Trevor. "You know, we will need to take care of Snowbird before we can go in for dinner—the rule is you always take care of the horse first before you take care of yourself. Let's give her a quick brush job and then we can go get cleaned up for dinner."

As they headed for the house, Peggy was inside telling her dad that Trevor had no right to put Annie on a horse. She could have gotten hurt. "Peggy, you were riding your own pony at Annie's age. You are way too overprotective—Trevor was being incredibly careful with her, as you saw."

The days went by, and Peggy did not seem to be in a rush to get back to the restaurant, which Trevor later learned she owned. Only being 24 years old she had done quite well for herself. The whole family noticed that Peggy did not seem in any rush to go home, and they loved it as they had more time with Annie—although it seemed that Annie was spending most of her time with Trevor. "Look at them trying to rope that post," Peggy said to her mom. "He is so good with her, but it won't be long and she will have to go spend time with her dad."

Faith also noticed that Annie was not the only one spending time with Trevor. Every time Faith went looking for Trevor, she usually found Peggy. A family dance was coming up in town and Trevor had already asked Peggy if she would like to go with him; she said yes. The whole family would be there, but Peggy felt special when Trevor picked her up at the door of the ranch house. Trevor was totally surprised at how beautiful she looked, and he took the time to let her know. she blushed a little and said, "You know it, cowboy." The dance was a community affair and both Peggy and Faith had the opportunity to dance with many friends from school and the community they had grown up in—what counted was the end of the dance when Peggy and Trevor danced the last several dances together. She let Trevor hold her as tight as he wanted and even let him steal a kiss on the last dance. On the ride home, she sat close to him and said, "Let's go to your place when we get home."

Faith had gotten home first and was watching for Peggy to arrive, to see what was going to happen. She was surprised to see Peggy and Trevor both go into his trailer. Peggy had been with cowboys before, but not one like Trevor. He was not just using her to satisfy himself—he was truly making love to someone he cared about, and she could tell the difference. Peggy knew she would always remember this night for the rest of her life and dreaded what would happen tomorrow.

The next day, Peggy announced she was going back to school at Oregon State University. Peggy had a life plan, and a ranch hand was not in the plan. She had to get away before she fell totally in love with Trevor. Annie would stay at the ranch with Grandma, and Trevor knew that whatever Peggy and he had nurtured would disappear. No one in the family knew why she made the decision, but everyone would benefit except Trevor, who once again did not understand what went wrong.

Trevor would stay until he finished his practical studies at MSU and would continue to be a father figure to Annie until he had to leave. With Peggy and Faith both at school, Trevor began seeing more of Alice Moore, the RN at the hospital. Trevor could now wrap a baby with the very best of the RNs and was about to get his certificate. Another talent he discovered was that when all of the babies were fed and wrapped up, Trevor would begin to play his guitar and sing a couple songs he had written and the whole nursery would go to sleep at the same time. Alice felt this guy was special, but she was not sure they had a real connection, as he was country, and she was city. The time they spent together was great, but the things they had in common were few and far between. Trevor eventually broke it off and the only girl in his life was Annie. Trevor had received his certification from the university that allowed him to volunteer in a hospital nursery and it was time for him to move on. He would now have to figure out how he was going to tell Annie he was leaving the next day.

Chapter 10

*A*t twenty-four years of age, Trevor was beginning to think his days of rodeo and perhaps playing cowboy might be coming to an end. He had exceeded all of the goals he had set for himself back when he was seventeen years old, and perhaps it was time for a new challenge. He had gone from being a young, aspiring cowboy to a truly grown man and a very good cowboy. His body had matured from that of a young kid to that of a fully grown man. He was starting to think he should settle down and begin to raise a family.

Today in Calgary, Canada, Trevor was at what he thought might be his last rodeo. He had never really been hurt, and what sense did it make to risk an injury or your life, just to please some crowds or make a lot of money for rodeo owners and their sponsors? The bronc busting was just about to begin and he heard his name called. He had generated a name for himself over the years and was considered one of the top three bronc and bull riders in North America, but that and two dollars would only get you a cup of coffee. There was a long round of applause as he climbed onto his bronc in the chute. As the gate opened, he experienced the thrill of the ride; however, he knew he would last the full eight seconds and probably win the event because he was that good. The thrill of the event was starting to lose its luster for Trevor.

The bull riding required more of his attention, but again he expected to last the full eight seconds and win the event; however, when he was removed from the bull by the pickup rider, the pickup rider's horse swung a little too close to the edge of the grandstand, smashing Trevor between the wall and the horse. When Trevor was released by the pickup rider, he fell to the ground. The pain in his right leg told him something was wrong. As he lay there, the rodeo medical team took a quick look and called for a stretcher.

Trevor could hear the ambulance coming and that was about the last thing he remembered until he woke up in the hospital. The doctor came into the room and said, "Good, you are awake. We are going to have to operate on your right leg. It is broken in several places, and we will have to insert a rod or two depending on what we find inside. Also, one of the vertebrae in you back looks slightly damaged and might require a screw. Do you have any questions, as we are heading for the operating room as we speak?"

"Will I be able to walk again?" was Trevor's question.

"That's our goal," the doctor said.

"Will I be able to ride horses again?" was Trevor's second question.

"First, we learn to walk," was the doctor's reply.

Trevor had been out of the hospital for about a month and in rehab at a facility specializing in the type of treatment he needed. His phone rang and Candy was on the other end. She said, "What's up, cowboy? I have not heard from you for some time." Trevor told her what had happened and where he was. After thoroughly scolding him out for not calling and letting her know what had happened, she said she would be on the next flight out.

Trevor said there was nothing she could do, so she shouldn't waste her time. She thought he really sounded down and out for Trevor Tremaine. When Candy arrived the next morning, she knew something was not right. Trevor could not walk without crutches, but worse than that was that he had lost his spirit—he was just not Trevor. It was as though he had given up. After visiting for a few hours and talking with his doctors, Candy knew she had to do something to help him out.

Susan saw the limousine coming down the driveway and wondered who it could possibly be—probably city folks that had made a wrong turn. To her surprise, Candy got out from the back of the Limo. "Well, Hi,"

Susan said, and gave Candy a big hug. "What in the world are you doing in this part of the country?"

"I came out here to ask you a question."

"Shoot," said Susan.

"Do you still have feelings for Trevor?"

The question caught Susan by surprise, and she asked, "Where is that coming from?"

"Just answer the question," Candy said.

"I will always have feelings for Trevor—as you know, he helped me learn how to walk so long ago."

Lilly, who had heard the question, said "Bullshit. She's still as much in love with Trevor as she was on the day he left."

"Well, here is my problem." Candy explained about the accident and that Trevor could not walk without the aid of crutches; but, more importantly, he has lost his willpower. "His spirit is gone. I don't think he will walk again unless you help him. I know he still loves you, but he is too proud to ask anyone for help."

"What can I do?" Susan asked.

"I want you to come with me to see Trevor and ask him to come back to the ranch. After all, you know something about learning to walk and maybe you can inspire him to want to walk again, because currently he has no interest," Candy said. Susan finally agreed and they took the limo back to the airport.

As Susan and Candy walked into Trevor's room, he stood and tried to walk toward Susan. He began to fall, catching himself on the small table next to his chair. Susan came to Trevor and helped him stand up and gave him a huge hug that seemed to last forever. She said, "I hear you are having a slight problem trying to walk, so Candy and I would like you to come to the ranch for a little R & R. Perhaps I can help you with this walking thing, as I had a good teacher."

At first Trevor would not hear of it, but after a couple hours the girls loaded him and his luggage into the limo and headed toward the ranch. The girls got Trevor to settle in one of the downstairs bedrooms, even though Trevor wanted to stay in the loft. "You're not ready," said Susan. "Perhaps that can be one of your rewards."

"What are you talking about?" Trevor said. Candy excused herself and headed for the airport.

John and Lilly had arrived from town and were glad to see Trevor; they told him dinner would be at five p.m. Susan said, "All right cowboy, I will expect you to be up for breakfast at daylight and we will see if we can improve your walking."

"I don't think so," was Trevor's reply. "No reason to get up early."

Susan said, "You're not here on vacation. We need to set goals and rewards. I expect you to be shoveling manure in a couple weeks and to take me to the fall dance at the end of summer, so we you need to get to work."

"I don't think so," was Trevor's reply. Trevor thought for a moment and then said, "What kind of rewards?"

"You'll just have to wait and see," Susan said.

Trevor made it in time for breakfast, and after, Susan said, "Let's head to the barn and see if we can agree to some goals." She wanted Trevor to walk four stalls down, to where she had placed his crutches. Trevor said it was a waste of time as he did not think he would be able to walk again.

"I can't do anything," Trevor said. "If you can make it, you get a kiss." She turned her back and walked from the barn to do another chore outside.

Trevor made it to his crutches with a little help from the stalls. He thought to himself that this first goal seemed a little easy and convinced himself that Susan just wanted to kiss him. He thought this might be fun. He came out into the yard in front of the house using his crutches. He got his kiss, which seemed to last forever.

He tried for a second, but Susan was too quick. She reminded him that a kiss needed to be earned. "The next goal is to walk to the end of the six stalls with minimal touching of the top of the stalls."

Trevor said, "Boy, that will really be hard. I don't think I can do that."

"The reward will be another kiss and you can move back into the loft."

"Susan, I really don't think I can do six stalls. You're asking too much."

"Whatever you think Trevor, but I am not going to sleep with you in the house." She turned and walked away with a big smile on her face.

Trevor said, "Hey, wait a minute. What did you just say?" Susan just kept walking toward the house with the smile on her face getting bigger and bigger.

Lilly said, "Come look, Susan—Trevor is trying to walk across the yard using just one crutch. Oh my god, he fell. Go help him," Lilly said.

"No," Susan replied, a slight tear in her eye. "Just let him figure it out by himself."

Trevor had laid on the ground in the hot sun for almost a half hour before there was a sign of movement. Tears filled his eyes; he felt so helpless. Finally, he started to move and eventually figured out how to get back up and with the help of his crutch, managed to make it back to the barn.

Every morning was a struggle for Trevor as he made one stall, then two, then three and finally, after about a week, he made it to stall six. Susan had intentionally avoided the barn whenever she knew Trevor was practicing his walking. Finally, at the end of the week, he told Susan he was ready for the walk. Susan watched and Trevor made the steps and eventually fell into her arms. She hugged him and gave him his kiss. "You know, Ms. Susan, I don't think I have told you lately how much I love you."

Susan did not know how to respond so she said, "Let's get your stuff moved into the loft."

That night Susan told her mom what Trevor had said and her mom asked her how she felt about that. She said she loved Trevor, but he had broken her heart once by leaving, even though she was to blame, and it was hard for her to give her heart to him again. "I need to know I can trust him with it, and that he won't hurt me again."

"You do know he is a cowboy," Lilly said. "You were both so young the first time around. You both needed to grow up and you both have—perhaps you both want the same thing now? You know...marriage, a family, a ranch of your own. You need to sit down and talk."

Candy checked in with Susan every week and Susan gave a progress report. Susan said, "Trevor is getting more like himself every day. I think in another month he will be walking without the crutches and perhaps riding a horse."

Candy, hearing the excitement in Susan's voice said, "You are falling in love with him again, aren't you?"

"I have always loved him," Susan said. "It's just trusting him with my heart again is difficult."

Well, the month had passed, and Susan was correct: Trevor was walking with a cane and wanted to go for a horseback ride with her. Susan said, "Don't wear yourself out, as I am planning on spending the night in the loft and I don't want you to be to be tired. I want you to be able to pay attention to me."

Trevor said, "Don't worry, I will never get that tired. Do you think we should take an afternoon nap?"

"Let's get the horses tacked. We are going for that ride you wanted to go on," was the reply Trevor got. Trevor could not wait for dinner to get over, do night checks on the horses, and go to the loft. Susan kept teasing him by finding a few extra things to do in the barn. Trevor kept saying, "Can't we do that in the morning?"

She said, "You're going to be tired in the morning."

Going into the loft was a little awkward, as they had never slept with one another. As Trevor unbuttoned her shirt, she was undoing his belt and unbuttoning his pants. They both fell into bed knowing that what they were doing was the right thing, as they were in love with each other, and it was time to share it. In the morning, Susan could not believe what a wonderful time she had the night before. They both missed breakfast, and someone had already turned out the horses. "What are we going to say to your mom?" Trevor asked.

"I am just going to tell her your walking is much better," said Susan.

As time passed, Susan and Trevor had their little talk about their future goals and the concerns she had about Trevor breaking her heart again. He promised it would never happen, as he wanted to settle down and raise a family. It was only one week later that Trevor went to John to ask his permission to marry his daughter. John said that it would please him very much if Trevor were to ask his daughter to marry him.

The next day, Susan and Trevor rode horses to Crystal Lake and Trevor proposed. She said of course she would marry him, and he slipped the ring on her finger. They hugged each other as tears of joy fell from their eyes. She felt like a princess in a fairytale and the dream was coming true. She could not wait to tell her mom—there was a wedding to plan.

Trevor said, "Why don't we just have dinner and see if she notices the ring on your finger? We can have a little fun with her." Susan went to the kitchen to get the plates to set on the table and suddenly there was a loud, earsplitting scream from Lilly. Trevor said to John, "There is either a rattle snake in the kitchen or Lilly just noticed Susan's ring." John said, "Well, I guess dinner will be a little late tonight."

As Susan and Lilly came running into the living room, Lilly said, "I should just throw something at you, Trevor. Keeping this type of thing a secret from an old lady is not funny." John said, "Let me see the ring, dear." Everyone was happy around the dinner table that evening, and all the girls could talk about was the wedding they were planning.

There must have been 400 people at the Running Water Ranch for the wedding. Barbeque, beer, laughter, and dancing pretty much described the reception until it was time for everyone to leave. Trevor danced most of the dances with his bride, as they floated around the temporary dance floor rented for the occasion. Trevor and Susan would leave for the Hawaii coast in the morning, as she had never seen the ocean. Trevor still had not told Susan about his life prior to working toward being a ranch hand, so they would have time to talk about their future when they arrived in Hawaii, as everything she wanted was now possible.

Susan was talking about how she would like to have at least one girl and one boy and live on a ranch close to her parents. "I know we will probably never have enough money to own our own ranch, but that is my dream."

Trevor said, "Well, we could start on the boy or girl tonight, but the ranch will have to wait until we get home."

"What do you mean when we get home?" Susan asked.

Trevor said, "We will contact a realtor and start looking at property as soon as we get home."

"I don't understand," Susan said. "How can we afford a ranch?"

Trevor said, "Remember you said you were in a fairy tale and dreams come true? There is one little detail I may have neglected to mention when you girls used to refer to me as the million-dollar cowboy. You were on the right track, except you should have referred to me as the multimillion-dollar cowboy. Money is not an issue in our life and anything you want is yours, because you trusted a ranch hand to take care of your heart. Now let's get started on our little boy or girl."

As the years went by, the love present on the Walking K Ranch was known to all in the county. Trevor and Susan went to many support groups to tell their story, in hopes that it would inspire others who had similar obstacles to overcome.

Chapter 11

When Trevor unexpectedly passed at the age of fifty-seven, life on the ranch slowed down a bit, allowing Susan to grieve and deal with the loss of her soulmate. Trevor's heart attack was totally unexpected. Susan eventually asked the kids if they should have a memorial for their dad, so that all of Trevor's friends could come and celebrate his life with them. Both Tammy and Tucker thought it would be good for their mom and could help her get closure—it was time for Susan to move forward with her life and again participate in the running of the ranch and the social activities of the community.

Susan knew that all the locals would come, as was standard practice, but she wanted to know more about Trevor's life before he came back to the ranch. Other than a few rodeo buckles she had found going through his things, he had never talked much about what his life had been like when he had left the ranch at the young age of seventeen.

Susan thought about it a while and told the twins, Tammie, and Tucker, that she knew just the person to organize and put the plan in motion. The kids felt good seeing their mom showing an interest in the memorial, as she had a hard time when Trevor passed and really did not show any interest in anything.

Susan made the call to the one person that knew all about Trevor's past life, Candy Wade. Candy told Susan she would be more than willing to organize the memorial. Susan asked if she could reach out to other friends that Trevor had known, in addition to a list of family friends that Susan would provide. Candy was not sure how far she should go, so she asked Susan if she wanted friends invited to the memorial that were perhaps more than just friends to Trevor. Susan said she wanted all friends invited.

On the day of the memorial, Susan was surprised at the number of people showing up that she did not know. "Who are all of these people?" she asked Candy.

"They are people that helped Trevor through his life when he was not at the Running Water Ranch." Candy had asked many of the out-of-town guests to bring old photos of Trevor that they might have so they could be placed on the tables to be viewed by all.

Candy pointed out Lou Hemsley, who helped Trevor win his first rodeo buckle. "Over there is Paula

Jackson, who spent a night in the back of Trevor's pickup watching the stars. You can ask Sunday Hensley about that, as she and Paula both fell for Trevor at about the same time. Neither were successful, as Jessie Slocomb came back to the Silver Dollar Ranch about that time, and Trevor was smitten with her, even though she was seven years older. Becky Clarino over in the corner stutters—Trevor took her to an opera house in Portland, Oregon, only to learn she was in love with a fellow named Robert Grey. Robert also has speech problems. They ran into Robert at the opera and Trevor made sure that Becky and Robert got together before he left town. That's Robert standing next to her in the dark blue suit; they are married now.

"Peggy Fuller is Nate Fuller's brother and sister to Faith. The younger lady with her is Peggy's daughter, Annie. Annie became quite attached to Trevor as a young girl. Trevor was sort of a father figure to her, and they were always messing around, doing lots of horse play in front of the barn and taking lots of trail rides. Trevor taught Annie how to ride a horse.

"These are some of the people that Trevor met until he came back to you, Susan. I believe most are here, except Jessie Slocomb, who did not respond to the invitation." Candy told Susan that Trevor never gave his heart to any of the ladies because it was not his to give. "It always belonged to you, Susan." A tear formed in Susan's eye and she thanked Candy for saying that.

Susan was surprised by the number of people in Trevor's life that she had never met. She asked Candy if she could invite these particular people to her ranch house for dinner the following night, as she wanted to get to know them and their stories better. She did not want them here one day and gone the next, as she felt they could not get to know one another in the short period of time spent at the memorial.

Chapter 12

Cassidy had found two letters addressed to Trevor Tremaine when his mom, Jessie Slocomb, had passed. He did not pay much attention, as all they said was that she would like to have lunch with him so they could have a talk. Cassidy just figured they had crossed paths sometime during their rodeo days and just wanted-ed to talk.

When the invitation to the Tremaine memorial was sent to Jessie, it had been forwarded to Cassidy's address—this reminded him of the letters he had found a couple of years earlier. Although the invitation was directed to Jessie, the memorial was open to the public. Cassidy was familiar with the name Trevor Tremaine, as Cassidy had also done some rodeo in his younger days, and he often noticed that the record holder on many events at various rodeos was Trevor Tremaine.

Cassidy thought he would like to go to the memorial just to see who this famous rodeo cowboy was and maybe learn if his mom really knew him.

Cassidy and his family arrived at the building where the memorial was being held. Cassidy, a middle-aged young man of about thirty-six years of age, his wife, and a young child of about five years old entered the room where the memorial was being held. A gasp could be heard from a few of the guests and a hush fell over the room as the talking subsided. The young man that had just walked through the door with his family was a splitting image of Trevor Tremaine. He signed the guest book as Cassidy, Jody, and Hunter Slocomb. They began moving about the tables looking at some of the pictures.

Susan had become very faint and nearly passed out, seeing the young man. Tears began to form in her eyes. Tucker helped her into one of the nearby chairs. Tammy walked over to the guest book and came back, reporting to Candy that his name was Cassidy Slocomb. Candy had no idea who that was, but Sunday, who was standing close by, was well aware of what was happening. Jessie had brought her son to the Silver Dollar Ranch when he was about five years old.

It did not take long for Sandra and Sunday to figure out whose son Cassidy was. Jessie swore them to secrecy, but Jessie wanted someone to know in case anything ever happened to her. She had written a couple of letters to Trevor, but they were never sent.

Cassidy and his family wandered among the tables, not realizing that the room had gotten quiet. He finally spotted a picture of his mom and Trevor standing together with a horse in the background. Cassidy studied the picture for quite a while and tears began to form in his eyes, as he realized that the young man looking back at him in the photograph was his dad, the famous rodeo cowboy named Trevor Tremaine. Jessie had never told Cassidy who his real father was, but now he knew.

Cassidy looked up at his wife, Jody, and she could see the tears in his eyes. She said, "I think you have found your father." She began to weep with Cassidy as he stood up and held her in his arms. After looking at the photos, Hunter also understood what was happening.

Susan got up from her chair, wiping the tears from her eyes, and walked over to the Cassidy family, introducing herself. She said, "Let's have a group hug." Everyone in the room felt relieved and knew that everything was going to be okay. Susan said, "You know this is going to make me a great grandmother." Even after passing, Trevor had given Susan the gift of a new family, and especially a new grandson, for her to share her love with.

There was a lot of beer, wine, laughter, and tears shared that evening, and many stories were told. All were invited to Susan's ranch the next day as they all continued to learn about each other and their interactions with Trevor. Susan spent a lot of time with Hunter in the barn and around the horses. They went on an early trail ride, but finally it was time for dinner and more stories.

This was just what Susan had needed to help her move on—she gained a whole new family that she needed to get to know. Susan eventually grew as close to Cassidy as she was with Tammy and Tucker. They all grew together as one big family. Susan could also imagine the tears in Trevor's eyes—he would have been so proud.

Susan made sure that Cassidy would receive some acreage on the ranch, so that he could always have a place to call home, should he ever decide he wanted to move onto the ranch.

Today, Tammie and Tucker Tremaine are preparing cut flowers to take to their parent's grave in honor of their anniversary. Their twins now run the Walking K Ranch, which was composed of some 20,000 acres of prime cattle country. Ever since Trevor had passed, Susan and the twins had taken flowers to his gravesite—and now that Susan had passed it was up to the twins to continue that tradition.

They stood in front of the tombstones. Susan's had an inscription that read "I learned to walk for a kiss; I will love Trevor forever." Trevor's inscription read, "I learned to walk for a kiss; I will love Susan Tremaine forever." As Tammie Tremaine and Tucker Tremaine remembered the love they had been given, tears came to their faces. They hoped that one day, they, too, could find such a deep and trusting love in their lives.

About the Author

*H*arold J Reed, an authentic Oregon storyteller, weaves romance and resilience into the fabric of his tales. Born in the quaint town of Myrtle Point, Reed's migration to Albany at 19 only enhanced his repertoire of narratives. *While Walking For a Kiss* marks his debut in the world of novels, he's no stranger to enchanting listeners, having crafted countless bedtime stories for his beloved grandchildren. Today, surrounded by three children, six grandchildren, and four great-grandchildren, Reed continues to craft stories that resonate across generations, capturing the essence of love, adversity, and the human spirit.

Printed in the USA
CPSIA information can be obtained
at www.ICGtesting.com
LVHW021746170324
774499LV00060B/970